PRAISE FOR MARIA GRACE

Who hasn't thought Pride and Prejudice could use more dragons?

I've INHALED this series ... a well-written, well-researched, feel-good series ... this series is perfect.~***Kristen Lamb, WANA International***

I found it wicked brilliant!~***Jorie Love a Story***

I followed Ms. Grace down that rabbit hole as she truly held me captive. ~ ***Roofbeam Reader***

Leaves me in awe and delighted to have found it. ~***Ramblings of a Traveling Bookworm***

I was *still* surprised by how well this concept worked. .... It's by turns clandestine and tense, and playfully silly, and I found myself weirdly invested.~ ***The Book Rat***

SECRETS OF THE
DRAGON
ARCHIVES

By
Maria Grace

Published by: RBF Books

Secrets of the Dragon Archives

Copyright © February 14, 2024

Maria Grace

For information address author.MariaGrace@gmail.com

Author's Website: **RandomBitsofFascination.com**

DEDICATION

For my husband and sons.
You have always believed in me.

1
Chapter

September 30, 1815

"THERE IS NO DOUBT? You were indeed swallowed by a dragon?" Elizabeth asked. The dark-leather wing chair in her new Blue Order office was comfortable by any standard, but the urge to jump up and shake quicker answers from Sir Frederick Wentworth was nearly too much to contain. Had he any idea of the significance of his adventures?

No one in the Order's history had claimed such an experience as he had in Lyme. Being swallowed, then disgorged by the largest dragon ever recorded, and living to tell the tale, sounded like the sort of story one told children while visiting the shore to keep them from wandering to close to the ocean.

Fairy dragon April, her turquoise-blue feather scales pouffed, chittered on her shoulder. "The midwife said you were to avoid too much excitement."

Granted, that was why they had left Pemberley for London. Between the poachers that had polluted the shades of Pemberley, and the smugglers who had trespassed there, her nerves had been worn threadbare. Still though, the midwife would surely forgive her excitement at speaking to someone who claimed to have survived a sojourn in a dragon's digestive tract. Elizabeth sighed out a deep breath and settled back into her chair, laying a hand over the restless bump in her belly.

When she first arrived in London, she had tried to conduct business from her parlor in the quarters on the third floor of the Order offices. Not only were the corridors too constricted to accommodate larger dragons, but all the other warm-blooded officers working out of the Order's headquarters had their own formal, designated space. That she did not was an insult, not only to her, but to the dragons who had appointed her to her office. And that could not be borne.

So, what had been an odd workroom once used by the housekeeping staff, both warm- and cold-blooded, had been reworked into an official space for her work as Dragon Sage. Despite its humble beginnings, in every aspect of size, furniture, and decoration, it befitted an officer of her rank and status. Dominance had to be maintained, after all.

Thick, dark carpeting with some nondescript pattern lined the stone floor, and old tapestries that portrayed the story of Uther and Dewi penning the original Pendragon Accords, which had been retrieved from a little-used room in the library, covered the walls. Both helped warm and soften the space, preventing sound from echoing off the stone, though they still smelled musty from storage. Not even the strategically-placed dishes of dried lavender masked the stale odors. Mirrors and candle holders, fixed on the walls throughout, maximized the light for reading and writing. If there was one thing Blue Order designers could do well, it was maximize light in underground spaces.

The desk was really too large for her comfort but, since it was a dominance display, the dragons insisted it had to match what the other officers of her rank used. Not a battle she was willing to fight, so she accepted the desk. Still, though, she usually worked at a smaller table across the room, between the fireplace and the entrance to the dragon tunnels. Chisholm's standing desk stood near that smaller table. As long as those who entered her territory could see the hulking desk, the dragons who insisted on it were satisfied.

Three comfortable leather wing chairs, in various subdued shades of blue, formed a conversation cluster near the fireplace and bookcases. Those bookcases, which lined the two remaining walls, groaned under the weight of tomes borrowed from the Library and Archives, and there were yet more she needed to add. The office still had a way to go before it felt like it was hers, but in only a short time, she and Chisholm had made great headway.

Sir Frederick Wentworth, former naval captain, now magistrate of Lyme and Keeper to Kellynch, sat in a wing chair across from her and rubbed the back of his neck, shaking his head, as though he hardly believed his own story. On the floor beside him, his Friend, black tatzelwurm Laconia, sat back on his serpentine tail, bright eyes attentive to everything in the room. "No doubt about it at all. Anne, her Friend Balen, and Laconia witnessed the sea drake Chesil casting me up on the beach."

"It was quite the sight," Laconia rubbed his thumbed paw across his face. "We were uncertain at first if he was alive or not. He was covered in slime and bits of half-digested fish."

"Is it possible Chesil only held you in his mouth and simply carried you?"

"No, Kellynch tells me he thinks it impossible. He says that it is common among sea dragons to have several stomachs in which they carry food or, in his case, treasure. Something none of us will ever forget." He brushed an errant shock of dark hair back from his broad forehead.

"I have to agree. Kellynch bringing up the gold he carried in his belly to taunt Cornwall in court that day made for a memorable proceeding." She shuddered, and the baby gave a firm kick to her ribs. How close Cornwall had come to losing control and violating the tenets of the Pendragon Treaty and Accords that day!

"It did indeed. But, all things considered, I am quite certain Chesil swallowed me during the battle in Lyme Bay."

"I hardly know what to make of that."

"What do you mean?" Wentworth leaned forward, elbows on his knees, a posture emphasizing his lanky frame. "I am grateful for his intervention. Without it, I would not have survived. I do not understand, though, why whether I was actually swallowed is so significant?"

"While I am quite pleased with that outcome—pray do not mistake me—treating you as prey, swallowing you like food, is technically an act of aggression, or at least a bold assertion of dominance. But to have carried you to safety as he did is a mark of respect, a statement of openness to a connection. Conflicting messages, would you not say?" Enough to leave one with a sizeable headache. She rubbed her temples hard.

"Considering the long discussions after the event, I rather think it was the latter." Sir Frederick shrugged with a dark chuckle.

"Discussions in which Chesil asked for Wentworth, not that Wynn fellow who is representing the Order in Lyme at the moment." Laconia rose and placed his paws on Sir Frederick's knee. "Chesil claimed it was because of our connection to Kellynch, whom he considers his vassal, but I am quite certain it was a mark of favor toward Wentworth as well."

"All of that is both confusing and problematic." Was that really so difficult to see? She squeezed her eyes shut.

Darcy's voice in her head scolded: Not everyone views the world through the lens of the Dragon Sage. He was right. She needed to keep that in mind.

"The Council dragons appear to agree." Sir Frederick scratched behind Laconia's furry, tufted ears. "As a military man, I can see how divided Kellynch's loyalties might appear."

"Especially considering his rather rocky history with the Blue Order," Elizabeth said.

"So they have reminded me. I have no idea of how to convince Matlock, Dunbrook, and Chudleigh of his loyalty to the Order. If you have any suggestions, Kellynch and I would be most appreciative."

"It would have been helpful if he could have appeared here himself to answer questions." April twittered from Elizabeth's shoulder.

That could have been addressed in a more diplomatic, less draconic manner, but April was right.

"Sir Edward, the Lord Physician to Dragons, himself insisted that was not possible." Sir Frederick frowned.

"Absolutely." Laconia bared his teeth as he spoke, the tip of his tail slapping the side of Wentworth's chair. "Anyone who saw him would agree."

"Forgive my impertinence, Lady Sage, but have you ever seen the results of a dragon battle?" Sir Frederick asked.

"Only one. When Pemberley and her Keep fought Bolsover for her territory. After Bolsover incapacitated Darcy, she, and the minor dragons with her, took on Bolsover and exerted her dominance."

"I suppose that was indeed a battle, but I thought of it more as a duel. What happened in Lyme Bay was a battle by military standards, with many combatants and, I dare say, fatalities. Not unlike what I experienced at sea during Napoleon's time." He spoke the name in a low growl that Laconia echoed. "It also reminds one of the days before the Accords, when dragon battles were commonplace."

Elizabeth shuddered. "We cannot risk returning to those days."

"If Chesil had not stepped in when he did, Kellynch and I would have been among the dead." The finality of his tone left no room for further comment.

"Had that happened, the Order would have been drawn into the matter because of the attack on their own." Her stomach flipped, and she swallowed back bile. "Could that be why Chesil intervened?"

"In part. But as I understand matters, involving me—or perhaps any of the warm-bloods—was a step too far. The serpent-whales exceeded the authority Chesil had granted them as vassals in his territory. Hence his actions to remove them from his territory. One can hardly fault him for doing so, no?"

"Of course, he was right to do so. I did not mean to imply otherwise. It is what any landed dragon would have done." If Blue Order minor dragons had behaved that way, there would have been no way to avoid bloodshed. And where such a thing might stop was beyond Elizabeth's ken. "So many implications in this encounter, though. It is going to be difficult to sort out."

"The Council seems perturbed. Or at least they did when they spoke with me. But I suppose that could have been their annoyance at having to deal with a lesser warm-blood." He shrugged, not with annoyance, but a refreshing self-effacement never found among the cold-blooded.

"You have a talent for understatement, sir."

"They are not unlike large, agitated naval officers, though with scales, fangs, and claws." He glanced at Laconia with raised brows. "They have the same desire to hold many meetings and issue orders."

"But they are far more likely to threaten to eat you than any of the officers in our acquaintance." Laconia licked his thumbed paw, flashing his long claws.

"They are especially fond of issuing orders." Elizabeth chuckled. "Do you think you might have time, amid all the many meetings, to write the details of your encounters with Chesil?"

"I am no writer, Lady Elizabeth."

"Consider it a military report, then. Material I can draw from in writing a paper on the experience of dragon aggression."

"You are writing such a paper? Forgive me for asking, but it seems strange that you, the Dragon Sage, would have had such an experience."

"Unfortunately, I have." Elizabeth dodged his gaze. "Not so much with minor dragons, to be sure. But certain situations rendered Longbourn cranky, and ... well, enough said. Much as I dislike it, it seems the sort of thing that needs to be added to the Order's records."

"I would like to hear about your experiences, if, of course, you are willing to speak of them."

"I can hardly refuse, but I will have to beg off for now as the Council has summoned me. We will come back to the matter soon, though. Perhaps after you have begun your own memoir of your experience."

"Do I hear a bribe, Lady Sage?"

"If it is motivational, yes."

ELIZABETH CLOSED THE NEWLY-DECORATED office door on the first underground level of the London Order office building and stared at it. Barwines Chudleigh herself had designed the door, taking great pride in unveiling it to Elizabeth only two days ago.

A pair of carved and painted wyverns, wings extended, held a silver shield engraved with the image of a Grecian-style owl perched on a pile of books. Utterly unique and fitting, for so many reasons, it might have been Elizabeth's favorite part of the room.

No, it definitely was.

The long, familiar walk to the conclave floor, several levels below her office, had once been fraught with anxiety and anticipation. Dimly lit, dragon-musky stone halls and stairs, lined with painted images of cranky predecessors, both human and dragon, neither welcoming nor inviting to traverse. Now they felt as familiar as the path to the formal dining rooms at Pemberley. If she were absolutely honest, at first, that path at Pemberley had been every bit as anxiety-provoking as the ones in the Order office.

How many lifetimes ago had that been? How much had changed since she had helped Darcy recover Pemberley's egg? Which had led to her betrothal, and marriage, and motherhood. To her being named Dame Commander in the Pendragon Order. To becoming the Dragon Sage. How many lives had she lived in that short time?

How many dragons had she met since then? How many Keepers and Friends? How much had she learned since being junior Keeper to Longbourn? Hopefully, it would be enough for today.

The final stairway ended in a short corridor that opened into the great courtroom. Brutus, the massive jet-black guard drake, stood in the doorway, little black tatzelwurmling May dangling from his mouth by the scruff of her neck.

Heavens, what now?

"I expect there is some reason for your meeting me here like this? Which one of you would like to explain?" Elizabeth placed her hands on her hips and flared her elbows, reminding both of them she was 'big.'

"The little one has been out of safe territory." Brutus grumbled, settling Little Anne's Friend on the stone floor.

"No one forbade me to use those tunnels." May craned her neck to lick her rumpled scruff fur, as offended as any warm-blooded cat might have been at such ignoble treatment.

"Which tunnels?" Elizabeth said.

"The one near the Council chambers." Brutus stared at May and growled softly—not a threatening growl, but more like the voice Mrs. Sharp used when Little Anne willfully disobeyed.

"You know better than that, May. Why were you there?"

"There is no rule against it. I have violated no territory claims nor disobeyed any direction from you."

"Why were you there?"

"Perhaps an issue of dominance?" Brutus prodded May with his elbow.

"Everyone here believes that the minor dragon who knows the most is the most powerful." May's fur stood on end, and she puffed out her chest. One had to admire her pluck, trying to be big in such company. "Who does not want to be dominant?"

Fairy dragon feathers! As though she needed another complication. "Listen to me carefully, May. If there is one place you do not want to be caught up in dominance games, it is here. There are far older, cannier dragons playing them here. You stand no chance of winning, and stand a very good chance of getting hurt."

"You do not trust me." May slumped into a pout.

"No, I do not trust them. That is an important distinction you need to remember. Now listen to Brutus, and do as he says." Elizabeth crouched to scratch under May's chin. "Do not cross paths with the Council dragons. But whatever you hear elsewhere, in the places where it is wise for you to walk, bring it to me immediately, yes? It is my job to understand what is going on between warm- and cold-bloods and I rely on your help to do so."

"So even though we are small, we are important to you?" May looked up, her golden eyes wide.

"Yes, all of you are. Size is not the only thing that makes one important. Now I must get on to meet with the Council. Keep away from trouble. Understood?" Elizabeth heaved herself back to her feet. Gracious, that was getting hard to do.

"Yes, Lady Sage." May stretched her front feet out and touched her chin to the floor, purring. Silly little thing was still very much a wyrmling despite her almost-adult size.

"I will keep watch over her." Brutus nudged May with his long, toothy snout.

Theirs was a unique relationship, part friend, part guardian, with issues of dominance tied up somewhere in there as well. One more unexplored, unexpected aspect about dragons Elizabeth needed to better understand. But that was for later.

Only a few torches had been lit within the courtroom, providing just enough light to walk across the wide floor, the width of four substantial ballrooms, to the largest of the dragon tunnel entrances. How her footsteps echoed against the walls, getting lost in the darkness and vast height above. How empty, alone, and insignificant she felt surrounded by the cold, stone-scented emptiness. That had probably been intentional in its design. A reminder to all, warm- and cold-blooded, that they were but an insignificant piece in the totality of the Order.

A pale blue minor drake, with a dainty head frill and long tail that ended in a bony knob, wearing an Order badge, standing on her back legs, met her there. "Good day, Lady Sage." She dropped to all fours, front feet extended, chin on the ground.

Elizabeth tapped the back of the drake's head. "The Council is ready for me?"

The drake rose to her hind feet with a dancer's grace. "They are, Lady. If you will come with me, I will announce you to them."

"Lead on." Elizabeth walked several steps behind the drake to stay out of the path of her lithe, swaying tail.

Few warm-bloods had ever traversed this tunnel to the private chamber where the Dragon Council met. It was the one that the more important dragons used to enter the courtroom, the only one large enough to accommodate the great firedrakes like Matlock, Cornwall, and Buckingham. Not a space where warm-bloods were welcome.

Had Lord Matlock ever been invited here? Hard to say, but not something she would ask, or even mention. Lord Matlock tended to be prickly where Elizabeth and the Council dragons were concerned.

Only just enough torches lit the way. Just enough that Elizabeth could make out the floor in front of her. Just enough that the darkness did not close in around her. Just enough that she could not be certain whether that shadow at the corner of her eye was something to be feared or not.

Just enough to be interrupted with painful brightness pouring from an open door.

The drake stopped in the brightness and peeked in. "The Lady Sage, Cownt Matlock."

"Enter." The rock beneath her feet rumbled with Matlock's bellow.

The drake shut the door as she scurried away, leaving Elizabeth alone to her fate.

Any room large enough to hold three major dragons would have been considered huge. This one would have comfortably accommodated six. It held no furniture; dragons needed no such accommodations. Likewise, the rough-hewn walls were devoid of any decoration or softness. The far side of the oval-shaped space ended in a tunnel opening. A second exit was a necessary feature—major dragons always needed a ready escape, especially when dealing with sensitive matters.

Extra torches had been added, probably for her benefit. Most dragons saw as well in the dark as she did during the day. It was kind of them to consider the limitations of her puny warm-blooded form. Dragon musk, rock dust, and tension hung in the air like the evening fog, cool and foreboding.

Cownt—more properly Grand Dug, but for political reasons he and Lord Matlock downplayed that as much as possible—Matlock stood in the center of the room, nearest the second exit, wings folded over his back. His shining blue-green hide shone in the flickering torchlight. The tips of his fangs and the whites of his eyes were barely visible in the shadows of his face. Not a good sign.

To Matlock's right, major drake Barwin Dunbrook hunkered down like a cat watching a mouse. His stony-grey hide had a dusty finish, while everything about him seemed squared-off and severe. With a face carved into a permanent scowl and a voice to match, he radiated displeasure even when pleased.

Barwines Chudleigh, on Matlock's left, seemed entirely out of place. A graceful, jade green amphithere with a lithe snake-like body, powerful iridescent-feathered wings and a stunning feathered headdress, she was the lone dragon who furnished her lair, and did so with down-filled pillows chosen for their comfort and beauty. Nothing about her felt like it belonged in rough-hewn caverns, not even her sweet floral musk.

Elizabeth strode several steps into the room and dropped nearly to the floor, arms overhead, fingertips touching the ground. A bow appropriate to the three most powerful dragons of England. And one she would not be able to repeat until Baby Darcy made his or her appearance near the end of the year. They released her from her obeisance and beckoned her into the room.

"Honored Council, have you considered the issues I brought to you when we last met?" Nothing about that meeting had been successful, which was to be expected when dealing with cranky, preoccupied dragons.

News of Sir Frederick's experiences in Lyme had distracted Matlock and Dunbrook with the implications of the battle and Chesil's actions. Chudleigh, though, had considered traveling there herself to offer her venom for Kellynch's wounds. A magnanimous offer that correspondence from Sir Edward, carried by Balen, Lady Wentworth's new Friend, had since assured her would be unnecessary, as Kellynch's wounds were not of the type likely to benefit from the administration of amphithere venom. All of which was a great relief to Chudleigh, who liked neither the seaside nor giving up her precious venom.

"We continue to debate the issuesss." Chudleigh ended the statement with a hiss.

Which was to say they had given minor dragons' rights no further discussion and would be happy for her to leave the matter lie—permanently.

"Do not inquire again. We will inform you when we are ready for that discussion," Dunbrook muttered through gritted teeth.

Elizabeth curbed her urge to argue. Today she would abide by those wishes. But only today. He was well aware she would not drop the topic so easily, but no harm in preserving his dignity for now.

Matlock growled a throat-clearing sound and raised his head a little higher. "There are other serious matters which we require you to address."

What now? Was the kingdom falling apart at the seams? "What are your concerns, Cownt?"

The three dragons looked at each other in a silent conference of facial twitches, tail flicks, and chest-puffing she could barely follow.

"Have you met with the Historian sssince your return?" Chudleigh asked.

Unexpected. Strange. "I have dined with him once and had tea with him on another occasion."

"But have you met with him?" Dunbrook scratched at the rock floor, leaving gouges under his front foot.

The baby kicked and turned, not appreciating the dragon's tone. "If you mean have I discussed anything more than the weather and his health? No, I have not. As I understand, he is busy with a new project."

"That is what we are concerned about," Dunbrook said.

"The translations he is working on? I do not understand why they might bring you concern."

"His new assistant. The one you sssent." Oh, that was a dangerous tone of voice from Chudleigh.

"Bede? He has not mentioned that she has been a problem. I realize she is difficult, and she does not comprehend dominance well—"

"That is not the problem." Chudleigh slapped the floor with her tail.

"You want me to intervene with her?" Not that it would be helpful, considering Elizabeth had been unable to accomplish any change in Bede during her time at Pemberley, no more effective, and possibly less so, than Mrs. Fieldings' school had been.

"Her ssstubbornness and determination are problematic."

"What has she done? She was supposed to be helping the Historian with some manuscripts from the oldest part of the archives."

"She has been digging in the oldest parts of those archives." Matlock's thundering voice echoed from the walls, like knitting needles shoved into her ears.

Was it possible for the baby to be turning somersaults in her belly? She wrapped both hands around her middle and pressed. Perhaps that would soothe the baby. "Digging? Do you mean combing through the old documents?"

Dunbrook rose from his crouch. "No, we mean literally digging—"

"We have heard she has created new tunnelsss in the oldest part of the Archives."

"Are Bede's actions threatening the stability of the office structure?" Elizabeth glanced at the ceiling. There were moments like this when the panic of being so deep underground surged forward like a pack of angry dogs, threatening to overwhelm her.

"No. Even she can sssense the ssstate of the earth and rock. That is not the problem."

"Why is she digging? Some drakes have an unfortunate nervous habit of digging where they should not. If that is the case—"

"That is not the problem," Dunbrook said.

"Then why is she digging?"

Matlock lifted his wings, enough to remind them all he was bigger. "She believes that there might be additional rooms, unknown rooms, in the archive complex."

New rooms in the archives? That was the sort of thing Papa both dreamt about and dreaded. New information had a nasty way of being a double-edged sword. She rubbed down the prickling hairs on the back of her neck. "Has she found anything?"

"We do not know." An angry thump of Matlock's tail punctuated the statement.

"You do not know?" Elizabeth slipped back a step as she pulled her shoulders back and stood up very straight.

"The Hissstorian has made no reports to us."

"He does not report to the Council directly, though, so that is not unusual. If you are concerned, why not ask him? He would not dare ignore a summons from you."

Dunbrook snarled. "He values dragon histories over everything."

"You mean to say that you do not expect he will be honest with you? That he might hide something from you? That he has so little respect for your dominance that—"

Matlock sat back on his haunches and roared. Elizabeth fought not to cover her ears.

"Find out what Bede has discovered. Tell us what he is researching," Matlock said.

"What could he be working on that would be so alarming? There is no greater supporter of the Order than he."

"Do as we have asked. Find out what he is working on. Leave us to understand our business." Matlock dropped low and leaned into her face. "Go now and be about our business quickly."

That was an order, not a suggestion. Best not draw attention to his disrespect, though. Elizabeth bowed and retreated through the door she had entered from.

What could they be concerned about? What might Bede have found? Perhaps it was their uneasiness with Chesil. That made sense. Such a huge, dominant dragon on the outskirts of Blue Order territory would be enough to set any major dragon on edge.

Perhaps Papa was researching something about the sea dragons and was not willing to talk with them about it until he fully understood the matter. He often did that, much to Elizabeth's frustration.

Then again, it might be yet another problem caused by Bede just being Bede. With no instinctive sense of dominance or propriety, nor any control over her tongue, the little black and white drake was forever causing strife and offense wherever she went. Perhaps it was too much to hope that working with Papa, the Order's Historian, would be the one place Bede could fit in.

In any case, the matter was a timely reminder that she had many questions about sea dragons. An excellent reason to pay a call on Papa.

2
Chapter

She made the breathless climb upstairs. Gracious, it seemed to grow more difficult each day. At least the movement seemed to lull the baby into the quietude she needed to face Papa. Though the stairs were no obstacle to her, April chose not to join her. Papa's temper wore on her, and she was in no mood to curb her urge to nip ears.

Late-morning light filtered through the frosted windows along the hall, amplified by strategically-placed mirrors to render the corridor even brighter than it would have been with normal windows to admit the sun. That same sun warmed the space, making it one of the most comfortable areas of the offices which, on the whole, leaned toward cool and dank as the colder, dragon-musk-tinged air from the basement levels filtered in through the staircases.

The Historian's door stood ajar, but Elizabeth knocked anyway. Papa had been more than prickly since her installation in a downstairs office, with access to the dragon tunnels and a properly ornate door, in such short order. He did not like reminders that his daughter held an office in the Order especially created for her, or that her office had all the appearances of greater prestige and, dare she say, dominance, than his. Though she could understand his irritation–dragons never like reminders of their place in the order of things–that did not mean she enjoyed the reality of it. Or the tiptoeing required to keep his pride mollified, a distinctly warm-blooded practice that no cold-blooded dragon would ever bother with.

"Ah, yes, Lizzy," Papa called, shuffling up to her, walking stick clacking on the stone floor, as he stepped out of his office to join her in the corridor. The tart edge to his voice suggested he had not drunk enough willow bark tea today. Perhaps with Sir Edward's absence, it was being neglected. Something to ask Drew about. "I was wondering how long it would take you to put forth the effort to call upon the Historian in an official capacity. Too busy with your own official duties, I imagine?" He raised an eyebrow and stared at her, as though waiting for her to take up the bait he had thrown her. When she did not, he wrinkled his face into a disagreeable knot. "I suppose you are expecting an escort to the Archives."

Elizabeth sucked in a deep breath and bit her tongue. He was the same Papa that he had always been. Most would consider him bordering on rude and insensitive. Even within the Order, he was regarded as one of the most draconic-tempered men. But he was who he was, and nothing was going to change.

As he was oblivious to his rudeness, one could not take it personally. Or at least they should not. So, the best alternative was to take him in small doses, rather like his willow bark tea. "Well, I am here now and hoping that you can help me locate information on sea dragons. The official library provides little insight."

"So, you've been talking to Wentworth as well, have you? I expected as much. I imagine you've already instructed him to write some sort of record or another."

"Yes, he will grace us with his writings—"

"Grace us?" Papa rapped his walking stick on the stone floor. "He said that? It is a privilege and a duty to add to our collection of dragon lore. How dare he—"

"Calm down, Papa, please. He is in no way arrogant. I was merely being light-hearted about a heavy subject."

"I have taught you better than to take such matters lightly, Lizzy. Your attitude will affront the Council dragons. Make no mistake about that."

Not yet invited into his office and he was already offended! Gracious, this temper was excessive, even for him. "When I spoke to them a few moments ago, they had nothing to say on the matter."

"That is lucky for you. I would warn you to step lightly. It does not do to provoke dragons, you know."

"Yes, I am well aware of that." Or had he forgotten Long-bourn and his inexcusable tantrum? Best not bring that up, though. Papa still blamed her for provoking Longbourn. "But about the sea dragons?"

"I have put Drew and Bede to work on the matter. They have pulled out all they could find and set it aside—waiting for you to come around for it." He cast her a vaguely disapproving glare.

She bristled, pulling her shoulders back and her spine straight. She was taller than he now, and he did not like to be reminded of that. "I imagine you have already read it all?"

"It is not my only task."

"I am certain of that; however, I am well aware of how you are when presented with the possibility of new information."

"It did not take long to accomplish." He sniffed and barely avoided rolling his eyes. "For your benefit, I separated it into two stacks, that which I consider useful and reliable ... and the rest."

"Hearsay, fairy stories, and drunken accounts of shadows in the dark?" She glanced down the long corridor, with its population of Blue Order portraits crowding the walls. Maybe that would encourage him to begin the journey to the Archives.

"Should I permit the information I consider reliable out of the archives, I expect you will not find it difficult to carry out on a single trip without assistance." He edged into a diffused sunbeam. Perhaps the warmth was the reason he lingered here in the corridor.

"That is disappointing. Not unexpected, but disappointing."

He harrumphed. "I hope Wentworth will provide considerable additions to that knowledge base."

"How is Bede working out? I had hoped she would find herself an excellent fit for your work in the Archives." She held her breath. Perhaps now was not the best time for that question.

"She is a remarkable specimen. I swear she is more stubborn than you. Always chasing down the most unlikely paths of research."

"It sounds as if that would be a good thing. Is her memory as impressive as I have heard?"

"Indeed it is, which, combined with her stubbornness, makes her a formidable force in research. But often it impedes accomplishing those needful tasks, which she finds less necessary or less interesting." He grumbled low in his throat, the way he often had with Elizabeth as a child.

Not a sound she preferred to hear. "But she has made herself useful?"

"I did not say she had not. We are growing accustomed to one another." He tapped his walking stick again and pulled his office door shut. "Come, I will take you down to the Archives."

It would have been easier for him to escort her to the library, on the same level as his office. Perhaps that was another source of his irritation, that she would require him to descend more than five levels of stairs and further levels of irregular tunnels to get to the Archives. At least this time, her gravid condition gave them a face-saving excuse to take the journey slowly, with many breaks to stop and catch their breath.

The deeper they descended, the narrower, steeper, and more irregular the stairs became. The air turned colder, permeated with the distinct smell of damp stone. How much longer would Papa be able to manage this trip? Maybe she should work with the minor dragons to find some alternative—perhaps a sedan chair sort of affair? Absurd as it sounded, it might prove effective.

Once they reached the courtroom level—her second time to-day—they followed the wall to the right, away from the dragon tunnel entrances to a rough-hewn tunnel opening blocked by a rugged wooden door that encouraged one to overlook it. Too tight for the major dragons to manage, but accommodating enough for warm-bloods and minor dragons—it was the understated entry to the Archives, arguably the most important space in the whole of the Blue Order. The rooms at the end of this tunnel contained the Order's oldest documents, many composed in dragon script. Ancient scribes penned nearly all of them, making those written in human tongues nearly as difficult to translate as those in dragon script.

So far, the Historian's and the Scribe's staffs had cleared and explored three rooms in the Archives. No one yet knew how many more chambers might lurk beyond those. For now, Papa and Lady Astrid focused on cataloging the contents of the three known rooms.

Papa unlocked the door with a heavy, dragon-headed key. He pulled a candle and fire-kit from his pocket and handed them to Elizabeth. She lit the candle and handed it back to him. The tiny flame provided them barely adequate light to pass safely through the narrow tunnel, if one were careful and took their time about it. Elizabeth had little choice but to do just that, considering she followed Papa, who hardly made quick progress. Between her own state, the close, brisk passage, and the stale air, she had barely enough breath to keep up over the uneven floor.

"It does not seem there is a great deal of interest in these old Archives." Elizabeth paused alongside him, both panting hard and leaning on the rough wall.

"No, not so much." He dragged in several shaky breaths. "But I am not sure that is a bad thing, either."

"Why would you say that?"

He turned so she could scarcely discern his profile in the wan light. "Knowledge is a tricky thing, Lizzy dear. Very tricky. It is neither good nor bad. Those things are a matter of what one makes out of that knowledge. And therein lies the challenge. What one may see as interesting, even helpful, another may declare dangerous, all depending on the perspective they take and the information at hand." He tipped his head back, resting against the uneven stone wall. "That means the information we find down here is at risk of being censored or even destroyed if it goes against the assumptions, understanding, or even the desires of powerful individuals."

A shiver coursed down her spine that had nothing to do with the surrounding chill.

"That is why I am convinced it is for the best that few come down here. It gives those of us expert at dealing with information an opportunity to clearly identify what is being said—and considering the age, and oftentimes the language documents were written in, meanings are not always as clear as we would hope. Once we clearly understand the text, we then may present it carefully, in the way it will be best appreciated and put to use. For the good of the Order."

"That sounds dangerously like controlling the situation for political gain." Botheration, she really needed to censor herself better.

"How dare you accuse me of such a thing! I am the Historian, not a politician. I never have been, nor will I ever be, such a creature. My goals are neutral in that regard." He turned to face her, his breath whispering against her face. "I merely want to know as much about the truth as possible and see that information disseminated to those who need it. Our goals are the same, Lizzy, to improve the understanding between the warm- and cold-blooded for the benefit of the Order. Make no mistake about that."

Their goals might be the same, true enough, but that did not mean—oh, so many things it did not mean. The baby kicked as if sensing her thoughts.

Papa snorted, tapped his walking stick sharply, and continued plodding through the tunnel. That he did not turn around and insist they go back suggested he believed she agreed with him.

Something she had not decided yet, but which did not bear discussion now.

He paused at the edge of a room-sized widening in the shaft that glowed with torch–or perhaps it was candle–light.

"What is she doing here?" Papa harrumphed under his breath.

"Who?" Who indeed would be so intrepid as to make their way in?

"The Scribe."

"As I understand, Lady Astrid is jointly responsible with you for the Library and Archives. Are you surprised she is here?"

"No, not surprised." His huff finished his sentence with "but I am annoyed with that woman in my territory."

Papa and Longbourn had a great deal in common. Decades of being dragon and Keeper had their influence, though neither was apt to recognize it.

A tiny, bird-like woman who seemed to contain the excited energy of ten active children, Lady Astrid sat on one of a pair of simple stools at a worn, lopsided table, hunched over a half-rolled scroll. Intense study was the only thing that could restrain her to such stillness, barely breathing, moving only to inch her glasses higher up her sharp nose or further unroll the scroll.

Papa cleared his throat, and she turned toward them.

She rose and picked her way across the floor, which was laden with stone-debris-laden, toward them. "Oh, Lady Elizabeth, I am delighted you have made it here." She swept her arms wide, gesturing to the depth and breadth of the space.

About the same size as Papa's office and every bit as jam-packed and dusty, rough, unfinished walls held torches on either side, marking the openings to the two other known Archive rooms. No mirrors magnified the light, so flickering shadows danced along the light's edges. Dust, ancient boxes, trunks, barrels, even a few large jars were piled haphazardly, left only a slender game trail through them. Framed paintings that faced modestly away from them lurked in the deepest shadows.

Elizabeth sneezed and rubbed her itchy nose against her sleeve. The smell of old books and documents always made her sneeze.

She had never seen a dragon's hoard, but if Papa was a dragon, this was indeed his hoard. No wonder he resented Lady Astrid's presence.

"Quill Driver, who should be about somewhere, can show you the sea dragon paintings we recently found. She can take you back to where we gathered the sea dragon material when you are ready. For now, you must excuse me. Bede and Drew said yesterday that they wanted to show me something." Papa tottered away into the darkest recesses of the space.

What did it mean that he had invited her into this secretive, almost sacred territory, then was leaving her alone with Lady Astrid? Surely, there was some meaning to be attached to his action. But what?

"Do come and sit with me." Lady Astrid led her back to the stools where she had been studying. The neat order of the nearest stack was a sure sign it was not Papa working there. None of the volumes bore titles on the spine. Bother! It would have been nice to get a sense of what Lady Astrid was researching. "Have you spoken with Sir Frederick?"

"Indeed I have, and I look forward to further conversations. He has quite the story to tell, and so much experience with sea dragons. And not only from the recent events. He and Laconia dealt with quite a few sea dragons. I do not understand why no one asked him to record his experiences before now. Unfortunately, I expect the Council will send him off to deal with other matters soon enough, so I have little time to learn from him."

"No doubt you have asked him to record his story." Lady Astrid knew her very well indeed.

"Of course. I suppose I am that predictable."

Lady Astrid peered over her glasses and winked. "That is not a bad thing. I believe dragons consider it a mark of trustworthiness."

"I will take that as a compliment."

"If I may, I would like to discuss that project with you." Lady Astrid chewed her lower lip. "Sir Frederick's story is dramatic, no?"

"Very dramatic, but that does not mean it is not an important one to preserve."

"But I wonder what more to do with it." Lady Astrid sounded like Papa. "Word of such things has a way of getting out, no matter how one tries to keep it quiet."

"Keep it quiet? Why on earth would anyone want to do that? His story is remarkable," Elizabeth said.

"Word of one of the Order being eaten by a dragon?" Could Lady Astrid's brows climb any higher? "Noteworthy, to be certain. But I fear that the news could spread alarm, even panic, on so many fronts."

"When you put it that way, I can see your point." Elizabeth broke away from Lady Astrid's piercing gaze. "You are concerned Keepers and Friends will begin to fear their own Dragon Mates because of it?"

"I hope not, but one never really knows. If not their own, though, then possibly other dragons who are less familiar to them."

"That's absurd!" Elizabeth tapped the table. She would rather have thumped it with a fist, but restraint was appropriate for a proper lady. "Every Blue Order member understands the Accords forbid such aggression. No Dragon Mate should ever be concerned about such a thing."

"Really, Lady Elizabeth? Really?" Lady Astrid let the words hover in the air like an angry fairy dragon, deciding which ear to nip. "What about your experiences with Longbourn and Cornwall and Bolsover and ... shall I go on? You yourself have experienced a great deal of draconic aggression, have you not?"

"Yes, but—"

"But you still have nightmares, do you not?"

"April has been telling Verona tales?"

Lady Astrid shrugged. "You know how fairy dragons are. She worries about you."

"I am fine."

"That is not for me to comment upon. But if you, the Dragon Sage, the one who best understands all things draconic, has nightmares from your experiences, then how might the common Keeper or Friend be affected?"

No, that was not something she wanted to dwell upon, which was why she kept much of her story to herself ... oh, dear. Was she now agreeing with Papa? Merciful heavens!

"Add to that how easily those same Dragon Mates might read Chesil's actions as aggression against the Accords...." Lady Astrid cocked her head and lifted an eyebrow.

"That is absurd. He saved Sir Frederick, not harmed him."

"Sir Frederick was eaten by a dragon. How fortunate that he rendered that dragon dyspeptic and was cast upon the shore."

"But that is not what happened." Elizabeth stood, knocking the stool to the floor behind her. Unfortunately clumsy, but better that than raising her voice. "Chesil rescued him—"

"Consider the means of rescue! Worse still, consider from what Sir Frederick was spared."

"A dragon battle in the bay," Elizabeth whispered, clutching the edge of the table.

"Listen to what you just said. A. Dragon. Battle. No one since the Accords were penned has experienced a dragon battle. What will people think?"

"That it had nothing to do with them. Why should they be concerned? The Order was not involved." That sounded more like a plea than a convincing argument. Maybe it was.

"So? They will instead focus on the fact that there are dragons about who are not part of the Order. And that those dragons are a threat."

"They have been there for many warm-blooded lifetimes and have never been a threat."

"But the Lyme battle turned against a warm-blood, did it not? It is not a far leap from that knowledge to wondering how many shipwrecks and other carnage and loss at sea might be the consequence of draconic interference." Lady Astrid slapped the table, rocking it a little off balance.

The Lyme Bay wrecks ... Sir Frederick mentioned Chesil had a fang in those. Dragon's blood!

"For the average member of the Order, the only dragons are Order Dragons. The Accords still govern even the 'wild dragons' of England. They have never conceived of dragons outside the Blue Order's reach. An idea aided and abetted by every officer of the Order, I might add. Consider how such a person would receive the news that there were other large, dangerous dragons out there, with no compunction against violence against warm-bloods?"

"It is hardly new, though. I have known about the possibility since I first became a member of the Order." Elizabeth's protest sounded more like an apology.

"Not to you, but you are far from the typical Dragon Friend or Keeper, are you not? We must carefully consider how to present Sir Frederick's experiences in a light that will be most beneficial to the whole of the Order."

"You mean rewriting his story to fit a predetermined narrative?"

"I did not say that. Surely, you must agree there are ways to present information to assist in a correct interpretation—"

"And who is to decide what that correct interpretation is to be?"

3
Chapter

THE NEXT MORNING ELIZABETH held Little Anne as she drifted off to sleep on her mother's shoulder and eased herself into the rocking chair which Mrs. Davies had sent from Darcy House to her guest chambers in the Blue Order office. Her own home, her own space, not subject to the constant potential for scrutiny would have been pleasant, but—how she hated that word—but, with Little Anne and another baby on the way, security issues were paramount. The possibilities were too ghastly to consider. Baby Darcy kicked her ribs hard, as if to agree that the Order offices were the most secure building in London, possibly more so than the royal palace. This was the best place for her and Little Anne and the baby to be.

Or so she had to convince herself.

She had been assigned the best guest quarters in the Order offices. Though her warm-blooded rank did not warrant so high an honor, her role as the Dragon Sage did. And the Council dragons insisted. For her to have less would have been an insult. Somehow, everything concerning her reflected on the Council dragons who had named her to her post. How tiresome—was this what it was like to be part of a royal family? No wonder so many of them behaved badly.

Though not nearly as luxurious as Darcy House, the four-room suite provided ample space for her, Mrs. Sharp, Little Anne, and their dragon Friends and staff. The largest room, a bedroom with an adjacent dressing area, had been turned over for use as a nursery and a bedroom for Mrs. Sharp. Elizabeth slept in the smaller of the remaining chambers, using the more substantial one as a parlor. The Order's housekeeping staff had shuffled elegant furniture, carpets, and decorative appointments from other rooms in the offices to furnish her suite. She recognized several of the parlor chairs as having come from one of the minor parlors downstairs. It was one thing to rearrange furniture in her own home and take notice of its new place, but here, it felt strange and uncomfortable.

Everything was of fine quality and impeccable taste, even if it did not reflect her own. She preferred simplicity to intricacy and comfort to formality, so it was difficult to settle down and relax in any of the spaces given her. Hence the need for her rocking chair to be brought from Darcy House.

Even with that, though, she often found herself pacing the floor, rubbing her arms, wondering what was missing. The Order offices had been so welcoming, so comfortable at one time. What had changed?

What had not changed, was the better question to ask.

She glanced at Brutus, sitting quietly in the shadows, unobtrusive, yet ever present in his watch over her. Though initially uncomfortable with his constant watch, she had grown accustomed to his presence, adding yet another dragon into their daily routines.

In the four years since she and Darcy had met over Pemberley's stolen egg, only her relationship with April, who was downstairs visiting with Lady Astrid's Friend Verona, remained unchanged. Every other relationship in her life had undergone some drastic alteration. Some for the better, some not. Some newly formed connections would last a lifetime, and some long-standing ones had proved unable to stand the test of time. Gracious, she had not looked at it that way before. No wonder life had felt so unsettled.

Little Anne hiccupped. Elizabeth patted her back and rocked. Hard to tell who the motion soothed more, her, Little Anne, or the growing bump within her whose wriggles and kicks were keeping her up at night. How different would it be to have another babe with them?

Thankfully, Mrs. Sharp already promised that she, along with Mercy and Truth, the valiant nursery zaltys who had the pluck to actually bite Mama when she threatened the nursery's security, would continue to serve the Darcys for as long as they needed. One could not overestimate the value of trustworthy staff, warm- and cold-blooded.

The nursery door slipped open and Mrs. Sharp walked in, her steps so silent that Little Anne did not stir. "Shall I take her to her cot?" Her bright green eyes reinforced her sweet Irish lilt. She was neither a large nor formidable woman, at least not by appearances, with soft grey hair and a gentle demeanor. But when she pulled her shoulders back and set her jaw firm, few were willing to cross her. Motherly through and through, but with the instincts of a mother dragon.

"In a moment. My work will still be there in a few minutes." Elizabeth sighed. "What are your plans for Little Anne today?"

"Verona has, with Lady Astrid's help, gathered a contingent of fairy dragons to join us in the nursery today. I believe April is helping her to organize that even now. It is remarkable how easily Miss Anne can hear their tiny voices. And they are delighted to chat with her, even if she cannot talk sense to them. Between you and me, I am convinced you are correct in permitting her so much contact with dragons. I have never seen a child so attuned to dragon voices and their mere presence. Sometimes I swear she understands what they are telling her. She has even learned some of their names. She tried to say 'Verona' yesterday, and you would think the King himself had addressed that little blue flutter-tuft—oh, the aerial acrobatics that followed!"

"I can well imagine. Perhaps you might arrange for me to take tea with Little Anne and her fairy dragon friends soon. How is May handling all the fairy dragons? It is a lot to ask of a young tatzelwurm to remain calm surrounded by so many flitter-bits." Sir Frederick had mentioned Corn and Wall, May's nestmates, had the unfortunate tendency to chase the local fairy dragons.

"She is a bastion of calm and good sense, and Mercy and Truth agree. Rather like her sire and dam, or so I understand. I heard tell that Laconia was a grown-up dragon nearly out of the shell, and I think May takes after him in that."

"We need all the good sense we can get, do we not? She takes a bit of time for fun, though, I hope."

Mrs. Sharp's eyes twinkled. "She probably does not realize I know, but often, when all of us have turned in for the night, she will take off, dashing about the chambers, eyes wide, looking for whatever she can chase. Mercy encountered her like that one night and found herself inadvertently pounced upon. Poor May was so mortified! It was charming really, how polite they both tried to be with one another. Of course, it was all good-natured, and no harm was done. And now both Mercy and Truth check carefully before doing their nightly patrols, to ensure they do not intrude upon what they call May's 'wyrmling time'."

What a sight! "I wish I could see that, but I will preserve May's privacy. A tatzelwurm's pride is as important as a firedrake's. I do so love to hear how well they are all getting on, though. There have been no few attempts to convince me that so many varied minor dragons cannot possibly live together under a single roof."

"Spoken by those who have never tried, I imagine?" Mrs. Sharp's eyebrow quirked as she tilted her head. How fortunate they had been to find a Dragon Friend so open to unconventional ideas to be their nurse.

"Quite so." The door on the opposite side of the room opened, and Chisholm peeked through. Time to get back to work. "I suppose I should turn my little darling over to you so she can get her nap before her visitors come. It seems I can no longer avoid what must be done."

Mrs. Sharp took Little Anne, still sleeping, into the nursery.

"I pray I am not disturbing you, Lady Sage." Chisholm scrambled to Elizabeth's side and sat back on her haunches, putting her head below Elizabeth's, but at a comfortable height to make eye contact as they spoke. Despite the light in the room, somehow Chisholm's deepest black hide made her difficult to see. It was an odd trait, but helpful in a secretary drake, whose presence was sometimes necessary but best unnoticed.

"Not at all. There is a great deal of work to be done, but I am tired." She pressed her hands to her swelling belly. How quickly it had seemed to grow in recent weeks.

"Only say the word, and I shall—"

"Yes, yes, you will keep even Cownt Matlock himself from bothering me. No doubt you could manage such a feat. But there is no need for that today. Pray tell me, what have you learned from the references we brought up from the Archives?"

"With respect to sea dragons or to the state of information preservation among the Order?"

Elizabeth slapped her forehead. "I expect we need to address that first before we deal with the latter. No doubt Papa and Lady Astrid are already painfully aware of the state of the Archives."

"Just because they are informed does not mean they are addressing the issue." Chisholm sniffed. If she had not been Elizabeth's secretary, she would have made an excellent assistant to the Historian.

"Of that I am well aware. You understand my father most astutely." Elizabeth folded her hands over her belly and rocked. The chair creaked a soft, reassuring rhythm.

"Ignore what is inconvenient and it will either go away or be eaten, appears to be the unofficial Order motto."

Elizabeth snickered. Unfortunately, Chisholm was right. "So, what revelations on sea dragons do the archives offer us?"

"I have taken extensive, cross-referenced notes for your use. But in short, the information is a typical mixture of truth, myth, and outright speculation. Regarding sea drakes, there are a few useful discussions suggesting that they play the role of the terrestrial firedrakes, holding the major territories and administering them as they see fit. There is no mention of a central governing body, though, nor any indications of how sizeable sea drakes might be, only that the largest dragon is the most dominant. In that, they are much like their terrestrial cousins."

"Are there any records of interactions between terrestrial and sea dragons?"

"It will not surprise you to learn that Cownt Matlock is interested in that same question. Very interested. Enough that he sent one of his own assistants to present that inquiry to me." Chisholm paused, allowing all the unsaid implications to fill the space between them. "I am aware of no such accounts. But that does not mean they do not exist. There are still many volumes in the library and archive rooms that have not been opened in generations."

"The mind boggles at how long it might take to sort through all of that." Quite possibly more than her lifetime.

"Indeed, it does, Lady Sage. Which renders the lack of staff for the Archives and Library even more notable."

Elizabeth pressed her temples. Papa and Lady Astrid made that same observation. Regularly. Just as regularly as Barwines Chudleigh, who oversaw such matters, seemed to ignore it.

"What of the records of warm-blood interactions with sea dragons?"

"Sorting between the flights of fancy and statements of fact is interesting. Until recently, I would have filed Sir Frederick's tale with flights of fancy. Considering his experience, I am starting back at the beginning and reviewing that material differently."

Elizabeth's stomach churned, and she tasted bile. Was that the baby kicking or the memory of Sir Frederick's encounters? "It is quite the shocking tale, is it not? Have you run across others like it?"

"Not nearly as dramatic. Small serpent-whales have periodically saved warm-bloods from drowning. That seems based on facts. Some of the various sea monsters sighted by sailors are likely to be marine wyrms or sea drakes, or even hippocampus playing tricks on sailing vessels."

"Much like we expected, then?"

"Yes, but I have a sense that if we study the patterns of the encounters, there will be new information to be gleaned. With your permission, I will work on that process after I finish going through the archival material." Was that a touch of smug satisfaction in the tiny twitch of Chisholm's tail?

"Excellent. Before you become too engrossed in that, though, would you be willing to work with Sir Frederick to get his story committed to paper before the Council sends him off again?"

Chisholm's shoulders drooped. "Will he be comfortable working with me? Many warm-bloods—"

"He is accustomed to a sleek black dragon who moves silently like you do. You and Laconia have a great deal in common. I am certain he will be quite comfortable with you popping out of the shadows with no warning." Elizabeth laughed. "I will meet with him later today and ensure he is expecting you."

Chisholm bobbed her head. "That is very good of you, Lady Sage—"

A brisk knock at the servants' door—the door the dragons often used! "Yes, yes, come in."

Chisholm crowded close to her as Brutus leapt from the shadows, interposing himself between the door and Elizabeth. Oh, the look of reproof on his face! She was supposed to allow him to approve all visitors before permitting them inside.

The door inched open, and Quill Driver poked only her deep-grey nose in. "May I enter, Lady Elizabeth?"

Brutus grunted and stepped back two steps. "Come in."

"Pray enter." Elizabeth added. "Is there anything wrong?"

"Not wrong, Lady Sage, but there are events of which Lady Astrid thought it best you that you be aware."

"What sort of events?"

"In the Archives, Lady Sage. Bede has been digging, and ... and ... please, come quickly."

"Allow me to lead the way." Brutus trotted toward the servants' door. His was not a suggestion and Elizabeth lacked the energy to argue.

Like most servants' corridors, the ones in the Blue Order offices were cramped, dusty, and poorly lit, and the stairs were narrow, steep, and uneven. None of which gave the dragons pause, but Elizabeth taxed their patience with her slower, deliberate steps.

It might have been easier, more pleasant even, to travel the main corridors, but there was also something nice about not being on display for others to take note of her movements and discuss them in whispered conversations outside of her hearing. The Order offices were like any great house in the kingdom—gossip flowed like water throughout.

At the bottom of the stairs, Elizabeth paused at the door leading into the great courtroom, panting hard, sweat trickling down the side of her face. She could not afford to be this tired right now. There was too much to be done. Blast and botheration.

"Lady Sage?" Chisholm nudged her elbow.

"I am well. Do not worry. It is to be expected."

"I comprehend little about gravid warm-bloods, but clearly, I need to. I will speak with Lady Dressler about that. She has birthed three herself and should be able to improve my understanding substantially."

Elizabeth drew breath to say there was no need, but there was no point. Nothing would deter Chisholm, and perhaps it was for the best. Elizabeth pulled herself up straight, and Brutus opened the door into the great courtroom.

Cavernous, dimly lit, empty, and cold, it greeted them with heavy indifference.

"Follow me, I have been entrusted with the key." Quill Driver led them to and then through the plain door to the Archives, stopping only to light a torch and lock the door behind them.

Had Papa locked the door when he took her in?

Brutus pressed tight to her left and Chisholm, on all fours, to her right.

"The floor is uneven, dangerous to two-legged gaits." Brutus muttered with more judgment than apology.

Dragons lacked a certain finesse when they were caretakers, but it was heartwarming, nonetheless. Overbearing, but heartwarming.

The flicker of torchlight at the end of the tunnel grew and brightened, welcoming them into the first room of the Archives.

Where were Papa and Lady Astrid?

"Come, we are not finished." Quill Driver led them to the far wall, where the torchlight from the adjacent walls did not reach. She pointed with her forepaw.

A nearly unnoticeable fissure opened in the unfinished rock wall. Another tunnel! A fourth room? Had there not been a bookcase there when she last visited?

"The Scribe and Historian are there."

The fissure was barely large enough for a man of Darcy or Sir Frederick's size to squeeze through. It was a wonder that Papa's hunched and twisted figure could pass.

Quill Driver stuck her torch inside to light the rugged, twisted passage.

"It is best if you place one hand on the ceiling, Lady Sage. There are places where the ceiling drops unexpectedly and you do not want to knock your head. Mind the floor as well. Step slowly as there are bumps and dips which can easily take your feet right out from under you."

"I do not like it." Brutus growled. "Is it necessary?"

"Absolutely." Quill Driver ducked into the tunnel.

"I will precede you. Place your other hand on my haunches. I will walk slowly." Brutus harrumphed and glared—a look no other dragon would dare direct to her.

He was probably right. "As you say."

Chisholm pressed close behind her, perhaps offering herself as a soft place to fall should Elizabeth lose her footing.

What might be at the end of this tunnel that would make this harrowing path worthwhile? Knowing Papa, it could be anything from an arcane bit of illustration of a heretofore-undocumented dragon type to world-shattering information that could change the face of the Order. Sometimes it felt like he revered both sorts of discovery equally.

Chapter 4

THE LAST TEN FEET of the tunnel proved the most treacherous, requiring her to edge through sideways, stoop, crouch, and use both hands and feet to traverse. How did Papa manage? As rapidly as she was increasing, she could not do this much longer.

"Where does it lead?" Elizabeth whispered.

"To the oldest Archive rooms. The material there has yet to be cataloged. The Historian and Scribe do not even acknowledge the official existence of these spaces."

The skin on the back of Elizabeth's neck prickled.

Candlelight flickered through an irregular archway up ahead. Was it natural or deliberately formed? Difficult to tell. Shuffling steps and hushed voices filtered toward them; was that the sound of claws?

"I have brought her! And Chisholm and Brutus as well," Quill Driver called, breathy and hushed.

The old air, with its thick, syrupy weight, pressed into the tunnel, heavy and musty, vaguely dangerous in its mystery.

"Bring her in." Papa's voice, thin and anxious, seemed still far away. Why would he be anxious?

Elizabeth's breath hitched and her heart raced as she crossed the threshold into the rough-hewn chamber.

"Come, come. Mind your step. The floor is uneven and dusty. It can be slick," Quill Driver said.

Brutus and Chisholm edged in on either side. She placed a hand on each of their shoulders. The only thing worse than a fall in this place would be trying to get out of here while injured.

The going was slow, though, and Elizabeth restrained the urge to rush. Something about this place demanded awe, reverence, care—it was difficult to put a name to it. But this room was extraordinary.

Quill Driver's torch, and one other wedged into a holder on the wall, cast irregular light to match the irregular shape of the room. Even in its unimproved state, this felt like a restricted portion of the Archive, but just how restricted? Who had once been permitted to study here? Who had even been aware this was here?

A few rickety shelves leaned against the wall near the torch. Scrolls, a few bound books, compact wooden boxes, and jars filled the shelves to overflowing. Dusty boxes and crates and chests in neat rows and careful stacks filled the rest of the space. Not placed in haste, but with deliberate intent. Interesting.

"I am so glad you are come." Lady Astrid rushed to take her arm. "They are not exaggerating the challenges of the floor here."

"How long have you known about this chamber?"

"It was only recently found and not yet disclosed to the Council, or anyone else. But it is important, more than you can imagine. We believe we found the first account of Uther Pendragon and Dewi's negotiations!"

"Original documents of the Accords?" Elizabeth gasped, leaning heavily on Brutus.

"Perhaps. It is still difficult to tell. The translation process is challenging and time-consuming. The documents are in dragon script, not any warm-blood's language." Lady Astrid chuckled with little mirth. The kind of sound one used to cover up something far more serious.

What did that mean? Surely, it was an important detail, but what did it imply? "Where is Papa?"

"Back here, Lizzy." The voice came from beyond a dark corner at the far side of the room.

Lady Astrid picked up and lit a candle and guided Elizabeth to a dark corner. "Bede has been assisting with the translations but got distracted, which ultimately led to this." She gestured toward a freshly-dug opening in the wall. "More tunnels, which had been intentionally covered over."

"Intentionally obscured?" Elizabeth leaned against the wall and fought to catch her breath. A room beyond this one, purposely hidden? How long had it been this way? "Why would that have been done? Is it not the dragons who insist that we keep records and remember all precedents?"

"That is what we have been told. It is not clear who bricked up these tunnels or if they were warm-blooded, cold-blooded, or both." Lady Astrid shrugged.

"Indeed? I am astonished." Well beyond astonished. Alarmed, anxious, even a little afraid. This simply made no sense.

"So, you have made it down." Papa poked his head out from the entry. His hair, his face, his shoulders were coated with fine dust. Trails of sweat coursed through the dust from his temples to his jaw. "The dragons were sure a woman in your condition could make it through if I could. I am uncertain if that is complimentary to either of us, but so it is."

"I suppose so. What is that room?"

Bede popped up behind him, her peculiar red eyes especially eerie in the dim light and dark surroundings. Her black and white hide, which looked like it was covered in shiny black and white glass beads, blended seamlessly into the shadows and rocks. "It seems to have been a storage room, not a proper library or archive, Lady Sage. Both the room you are in and the one beyond."

"The boxes and chests, some with writings, some with other artifacts that we have not yet cataloged—it is the find of a lifetime, Lizzy." Papa's eyes glittered, something she had never seen before. "It is the stuff one only dreams about in flights of fancy."

"And you found this, Bede?"

"The wall behind one of the bookcases sounded hollow to me." She dodged Elizabeth's gaze, ducking down a little behind Papa.

"She dug before I gave permission, to be sure. I would not have approved the activity without having carefully studied the maps and histories of the Archives. I would not risk bringing the excavations down on our heads." Papa glowered at Bede.

"But once I could show there was a passage here, as I knew there would be—"

"Yes, yes, then it seemed necessary to continue the excavation."

Elizabeth raised an open hand. "Did you obtain approval from—"

"From whom? Lady Astrid and I have the charge over all the libraries and archives. There is no one else to approve."

"But surely the structural issues of digging—"

"Are mitigated by finding there was a tunnel already dug and filled in." Papa braced his hand firmly along the edge of the opening as though to prove its soundness.

"Who knows about this find?"

"Only Lady Astrid and I."

And Bede, Quill Driver, Drew, and now Chisholm and Brutus, April and Verona, and possibly Bylock. too. And there was May who would smell the ancient dust on Brutus.

That was a lot of minor dragons. Was Papa choosing not to mention that or simply ignoring it for convenience's sake? Either seemed equally possible.

"It seemed best to keep this private for the moment until we can identify what we actually have on our hands." Lady Astrid clasped her hands before her.

Unfortunately, the Council dragons already knew about this. Should she tell them? "What have you found so far?"

"Those boxes on the far side of the chamber seem to contain a variety of items. However, these," Papa gestured to the darkness behind him, "are full of documents."

How much was there behind him?

"Many of them written in dragon script." Bede bounced on her toes like a schoolgirl.

"Ancient dragon script, which is quite different to more modern versions of the hand." Drew shifted from side to side.

"I actually find it easier to read. The modern versions take liberties with the letter forms and seem unique to the dragon who has written it, rendering so many variations one almost has to specialize in reading the script used by a particular dragon. Quite annoying." Quill Driver's tail lashed. "We are planning an initiative to teach a standardized dragon script soon. I expect that the minor dragons will be more amenable to it than the major ones, though. They are loath to change anything."

"That will be their loss, then," Bede said. "These texts are so much easier to translate than the ones in the other archive room. Look here." She reached behind her and picked a partially unrolled scroll and read:

In the year 900 as the warm-bloods reckon time...

Chills prickled like fairy dragons racing down Elizabeth's spine as Brutus helped her brace against the wall.

"If the scribe is to be believed, this dates back to the days of Uther and the initial drafting of the Accords." Drew's eyes widened in awe.

"But the exciting thing is this note here!" Bede's tail lashed as she pointed to a smudged patch next to the text. "It is difficult to read, but what I can decipher is 'persuasion' and 'agreed' and 'another date'."

"This hints at intentional use of draconic persuasion to establish a different timeline for Uther Pendragon, perhaps the earliest attempt to obscure traces of the Blue Order from the dragon-deaf!" Papa said, breathlessly. "Have you any idea how significant this is?"

"I can grasp its historical significance, certainly." However, its practical one was far more difficult to appreciate.

"It is not merely academic. It suggests a deeper level of human-dragon cooperation at an earlier period than we ever expected." Lady Astrid matched Drew's awestruck expression.

"The precedent set here could significantly impact the entire Order." Papa finished for her. "We cannot underestimate its importance."

Or the potential it might have for disrupting the Order as they knew it. No wonder the dragons of the Council were disturbed.

"That is not all, though. You will not believe this!" Bede pulled the scroll toward her again and read:

The current war has been going on for a generation of warm-bloods. The new breed of warriors among them are not like the ones of old. Different, hardened, more dangerous...

"This is an account of an actual dragon war! Perhaps the last dragon war fought before the inception of the Blue Order." Papa rubbed his arms as though chasing away chills. "We have no actual eyewitness accounts in the Archives."

Though the largest of the firedrakes, Britany, is convinced that he and his vassals will have control over the situation soon, Dewi is not nearly so certain.

"The scribe knew Dewi!" Quill Driver's voice trembled.

Firsthand records of Dewi? Dragon's fire! Had they found those fabled writings?

The last battle claimed many lives, warm- and cold-blooded. The loss of such numbers cannot be sustained, Dewi says. Major dragons do not reproduce like fairy dragons. Too many more battles like this one and major dragons could be at threat of extinction.

Of course, Britany does not believe it, but Dewi is quite certain. A number of the other major dragons are listening to him. A small and as yet quiet coalition forms under Britany's nose, which is open to seeking peace with the warm-bloods.

While Dewi is pleased with this, it is not enough. He seeks more than simply peace. He believes that cooperation may be possible. And that may be the only thing that saves both species from utter ruin.

Elizabeth gasped. Chisholm and Quill Driver helped her to sit on the nearest crate. "Dewi feared mutual destruction?"

"That is what this says." Bede hopped from one foot to the other.

Elizabeth pressed her fist to her mouth. "Does anyone else agree with your first impression at translation? You admit early interpretations can be problematic."

Bede handed the document to Drew with a snort. He took it and studied it, then handed it to Papa, who did the same.

"While I might argue with the translation of a few words, here and there," Papa glanced at Drew, who nodded, "we both agree with the bulk of the rendition. Dewi did indeed fear that Uther's forces might drive the major dragons into extinction."

Lady Astrid pressed her hands to her cheeks and sucked in a thin breath.

Dizziness threatened the edges of Elizabeth's awareness. "How is that possible? Our histories have all said—"

"Yes, they have all said Uther feared the dragons would wipe out his armies and the whole of humanity." Papa adjusted his glasses and pulled back his shoulders, as proud as if he had just now given birth to an heir.

"To think the dragons were similarly vulnerable ..." Lady Astrid whispered.

"It makes a great deal of sense, if one thinks about it," Bede said. "After all, what major dragon is motivated by anything but self-interest? If they had not believed the absolute necessity of negotiations with lesser creatures, they would never have permitted it in the first place, no matter how much they respected Dewi."

"Of course, of course. That is clear. But this is such a deviation from long-accepted beliefs," Elizabeth said.

"Accepted to protect the pride and dominance of the fire-drakes, especially. They have long believed themselves to be the most dominant species in England. Imagine what a blow it would be to learn they were so close to losing dominance here," Bede uttered the words as if she were discussing the evening's menu.

But Elizabeth shuddered. Imagine that indeed.

5
Chapter

ELIZABETH LAY ON HER tall four-poster bed, staring into the darkness that hung like velvet bed curtains between her and the ceiling. Bits of moonlight filtered in through the frosted windows, reminders of the different world outside her walls. The walls pressed in closer than those at Darcy House or Pemberley, but the room was sufficient for her use: to sleep, to dress, and to fret.

She shifted on the deep featherbed and propped herself on a stack of lavender-scented pillows. As the blankets fell away, chill air rushed in to take its rightful place against her skin. When she laid her hand over her swelling belly, the babe within stirred as though just waking. "Who are you, little one? Are you little brother Bennet, or little sister Frances? Do you consider it odd that we already know your name?"

April cheeped from her nest of soft in the white iron fairy dragon "cage" on the press across the room. She twittered sweet notes as she flittered over to land on the pillow beside Elizabeth. "The baby is Bennet, not Frances. I can smell that. And like the rest of you, he can well hear dragons." She chirruped at Elizabeth's belly and hopped a little closer.

The baby seemed to turn toward April's voice.

"You see? He responds to my voice."

"I am astonished you can detect—"

"You have no idea how acute my senses are." April fluttered her wings, her feather-scales fluffing.

"Why did you not tell me when I carried Little Anne?"

"You did not ask."

"In the future, feel free to tell me things you know, without waiting for me to ask." Elizabeth scratched under April's chin.

"Is that what you really want? I am not sure you will like it very much."

Elizabeth sighed and sat a little higher in bed. "Something about the revelations in the Archives?"

"There is a great deal to say on that matter, is there not?" April hopped back and forth along the edge of the counterpane. Was she pacing? "The first conversations need to be with the major dragons, not with me. However, you might need to pursue that conversation sooner than they are ready for it."

This was not what she wanted to discuss in the middle of the night, but then again, she had not been sleeping either. "You do not expect the Council to welcome the new records Bede has uncovered?"

April snorted so hard she skittered backward. "Hardly. Do you?"

"Not really. They can be construed as a challenge to the firedrakes' dominance, something that none of them will welcome."

"No, I do not imagine so. And it is not only the firedrakes who will be affronted. All the major dragons will feel the sting."

Unfortunately, true. "I must figure out how to soften the blow of that information, but it may take some time and study. Surely, this is not the first time their dominance has been questioned."

"I would not be so certain about that. And you may not have as much time as you would like. I do not expect that the news will remain quiet for long."

Elizabeth pulled herself the rest of the way up and leaned against the headboard, pulling up the blankets to recover the lost "warms," as April called them. "What do you mean by that? You are not a gossip. I pray you do not intend to become one now."

"You should know better than that." April hovered above the bed as though she were ready to nip ears. "I have no reason to meddle in their affairs, at least not now. But I am far from the only one aware of these matters. More dragons than you might expect are cognizant of what is going on. Not all of them will keep their peace."

"Can you, will you, suggest to them the delicacy this matter requires?"

"Those with whom I enjoy influence, I can try to persuade. But many will follow the lead of their Friends. Small dragons are not the only ones chafing under the rule of the major dragons. There are warm-bloods who would welcome the news as much as their minor dragon Friends."

"Who has heard what?"

"You have said yourself, there are always minor dragons listening." April perched on Elizabeth's knee.

"You do not know names or have an inkling of who might be privy to which details?"

"Not precisely, but that is hardly the point. Mark my words, the news is spreading as we speak."

"Without knowing who is saying what to whom, I cannot fathom where to begin. How does one manage such a situation?" Elizabeth squeezed her eyes shut and covered her face in her hands.

"Perhaps this is not a problem for you to resolve."

"What do you mean? It is my job—"

"To deal with relations between warm- and cold-blooded members of the Order. This seems very much a dragon matter."

"Be that as it may, there is no way that it will not affect the warm-blooded members."

"While that may be true, it does not mean that you are the one to manage it. Perhaps it is best to allow us to handle things in our own way. We have, after all, kept peace since the time of Uther and Dewi. Nine hundred years would suggest we dragons have some insight into these things." April hopped to her shoulder and cuddled into her cheek. "You need to sleep now. The problem will still be here in the morning."

How was she to sleep with news like that weighing on her chest?

April sang into the side of her neck—oh, that was how.

ON HER WAY DOWN to her office the next morning, it seemed every minor dragon in the office appeared to greet her—or maybe it was April, who clung to her shoulder. Probably her imagination, but it felt a little excessive—strange to be sure. There was something 'off' in the atmosphere, but she could not place what it was. Perhaps it was merely the stairs that seemed to grow more challenging every day.

The baby—little Bennet, as April swore he was—-kicked and turned as if he felt the disquiet, too. But maybe it was the rush of so many unfamiliar dragon voices all in a brief time. It was a relief to know he heard dragons, though. While there was only a slim chance that he might be dragon-deaf, the problems ensuing from the possibility were too overwhelming to consider.

Chisholm greeted Elizabeth as she walked into her office. The chairs had been rearranged again. This time, the blue leather wing chairs were pushed close to the fireplace and an unfamiliar wooden standing desk, a bit scuffed, stained, and canted to the left, crowded close to her own desk. April chirruped a greeting to Chisholm and fluttered to the little basket of soft on the mantel she insisted was necessary if she was to spend time with Elizabeth here. Cold still made her previously-injured wing ache and nothing helped her so much as resting in soft warms. How much more subdued she was since that ordeal.

"I hope you do not mind. I found the standing desk in a storage room and took it on my authority to add it here." Chisholm's head drooped a few inches. "It is rather plain—"

"But is it functional? Does it suit you?"

"Yes, Lady Sage. Quite well, in fact. I find it is quite the correct height and depth to permit me to write comfortably and efficiently." Her dark eyes brightened with a sparkle.

"Then it is essential, and I welcome the addition. I am glad you could find what you needed with so little fuss. We could order something built especially for you, but—"

"I prefer to have a desk now, than to wait the months it would take to design and build one fitting for the honorable office of the Dragon Sage." Chisholm chirruped a little laugh, the right mix of respect and reality.

"Along those lines, the head of the kitchen is now trying to craft a special blend of tea for me. I suspect she wants to enjoy the bragging rights for creating something expressly for the Sage." She closed her eyes and shook her head. "I fear the notoriety attached to my office is getting tiresome."

"It is an attitude quite encouraged in the London Order offices." Chisholm clucked her tongue.

"Often." April muttered from across the room.

"And ...?"

"It is not my place to say, Lady Sage." Chisholm murmured.

"It is, if I ask." Elizabeth crossed her arms over her chest.

Chisholm glanced over her shoulder. "There are moments I have wondered if making you a little less effective with all the excessive attention is an intentional effort."

"Well, that is an uncomfortable thought, is it not? But one I have wondered about myself." Elizabeth eased herself into the wing chair nearest the fireplace. What could it serve the dragons to interfere with her effectiveness, though? "Dare I ask what is on my schedule today?"

"I expect Sir Frederick will arrive soon. After that, the Council has politely requested your presence for a meeting—and no, they have not made me privy to their agenda." Chisholm fetched a footstool from under Elizabeth's desk and slid it under her feet.

Oh yes, that was better. "Not surprising. Would you arrange for tea and biscuits for Sir Frederick?"

"They should arrive in a moment." Chisholm smiled her bright draconic smile, still a little eerie against her jet-black hide. "Shall I take notes of your meeting with Sir Frederick? Do you prefer to use the desk or your comfortable chairs for that?"

"The chairs, definitely the chairs. Can you check the storerooms for some sort of cushion for my desk chair? I find the hard wood is not agreeing with my back at the moment."

"Immediately after your meeting, Lady Sage. Sir Frederick approaches." Chisholm trotted to the door and opened it to reveal Sir Frederick poised to knock.

He started, but blinked twice and regained his composure. Chisholm often had that effect on people—and seemed to enjoy it, though she never admitted to it.

"Do come in, Sir Frederick. Tea will be brought up in a few minutes." Elizabeth tried to stand, but April zipped to her shoulder, urging her to remain as she was.

"Thank you, Lady Elizabeth." He unbuttoned the last button on his jacket and sat down.

Gallant and polite in his own way, Sir Frederick lacked the polish and propriety that seemed to flow through Darcy's every breath. He was a handsome man, but in a more earthy style, worn and rugged, compared to her husband's noble bearing. But there was a great deal to be said for the earnest, confident strength Sir Frederick carried with him. His was a character one could trust.

"Forgive me for being intrusive, sir, but you seem a bit out of sorts this morning."

His lips quirked in a weak smile, and he rolled his eyes. "The Council dragons just dismissed me from their presence. They threw Laconia out before we even began."

"That can be a memorable experience. They can be overwhelming even to those most experienced in dealing with them."

"That would be one word for it." He rubbed the back of his neck. "May I share something candid with you?"

"Of course. April, will you ensure there is no one to overhear?"

April twittered and zipped several circuits around the room, checked the windows, the servants' door and even the chimney breast. "Your conversation is private."

Sir Frederick seemed to relax into his seat a little more. "Thank you, both of you. You are correct. The Council has left me with rather a lot to think about."

"What did they wish to discuss with you?"

"Cornwall and Chesil. They are most concerned about the impending conflict between them."

"Tell me more about that. I am still not quite clear on how a sea drake and a firedrake are in any position to conflict with one another."

"I do not think it has evolved to an actual struggle yet. That is what we are trying to avoid. Or at least that is what they say—I will come back to that. The stage, though, is set for a struggle. The long and short of it is that Cornwall has sought local sea dragons to teach him to swim. He is trying to claim a portion of the sea immediately beyond Land's End as part of his territory."

"Has this something to do with the Merchant Royal's treasure, or do you believe it is a grab of more territory to show dominance after his humiliation with Kellynch?" She probably should have brought that issue up with the Council after Cornwall's set down. Was it wrong to assume the dragons themselves would be attuned to such a thing?

"I have not heard the specifics, but I imagine both issues play a role. Kellynch offended him by taking that treasure, and he may be grasping at ways to ensure it never happens again. And there is the possibility that Kellynch did not take all of it. It would do his injured pride and sense of dominance good if he could collect at least a part of that treasure for his hoard."

"Not to mention such a feat would establish him as unique among the landed dragons. Something that would only increase his dominance in the Blue Order. As heir to the Brenin's throne, his pride and need for dominance are no small matters."

"Indeed, and that makes this all so dangerous." Sir Frederick braced his elbow on the chair's arm and shifted his weight as though to move away from the unpleasant truth. "I have seen Cornwall, of course, and appreciate his size and power. You must believe me when I say Dug Cornwall is nothing to Chesil. Chesil is larger than a frigate, at least twice the size of Cornwall, maybe three times. Any contest of dominance is pointless. Cornwall may learn to swim, but he could scarcely hold his own against a born sea dragon of his own size, much less Chesil."

"Like a gliding dragon challenging one who can actually fly, I suppose." Elizabeth laced and unlaced her fingers.

"An excellent comparison."

"Has there been a direct encounter between Chesil and Cornwall?"

"Not yet. Before I left Lyme, Chesil tasked me with convincing Cornwall to stand down and cease his claims to marine territory. If I fail, Chesil himself will resolve the matter. Between you and me, Cornwall would not survive the altercation."

"And the death of so prominent a dragon…" The dreadful thought triggered screeching alarms in every corner of her mind. "Have the Council at least offered to help you manage Cornwall?"

Sir Frederick's expression said everything.

"But why? That does not seem consistent at all." Not that Elizabeth expected dragons to always be consistent. That would have been unrealistic.

"It is as if they do not believe Chesil can defeat Cornwall." Sir Frederick offered a brief shrug. "I cannot fathom that level of arrogance, even from them."

"If they want to see Cornwall removed altogether…" April muttered.

Sir Frederick's jaw dropped.

"You cannot believe such a thing." Elizabeth blinked several times and forced her mouth shut. Surely, she had not—

"It would leave Brenin without a direct heir, and Matlock could then step into the role." April zipped back to the mantel and ducked into her basket, clearly done with the conversation.

"Matlock? He is not of Londinium's line. There is another younger Duges whom Londinium sired. No doubt she would be named heir in Cornwall's place, not Matlock." Elizabeth pressed her steepled hands against her lips.

"If I recall my English history properly, it would not be the first time a monarch was allowed to keep the throne in exchange for establishing a particular designated heir." Sir Frederick's entire face frowned. "I am thinking of King Stephen making Matilda's son his heir."

"That would imply Londinium—"

"… has kept a great deal from the warm-blooded members of the Order. Perhaps even the officers of the Order as well."

"I am afraid that opens up many uncomfortable, and even dangerous, questions." Baby Darcy kicked hard against the idea. Elizabeth smoothed her hands over her belly, as much to soothe herself as him.

"Even if Matlock's plans are as April suggests," Sir Frederick said, "that would still leave the Council with a grave problem. They cannot ignore a sea dragon capable of besting the second most powerful dragon in the kingdom lurking off the English coast. In either case, I expect difficulty of maintaining dominance in the face of that threat is what the Council fears the most."

"At least it should be," Elizabeth muttered. But perhaps she should have kept that thought to herself.

6
Chapter

Sir Frederick left and Elizabeth leaned against the door, resisting the urge to slide down to the floor.

"Shall I keep the notes from this meeting in the lockbox in your private quarters?" Chisholm whispered beside her. She glanced back at April's basket. That she seemed to put stock in April's suggestion was even more disturbing than April's idea.

"Yes, yes, that seems the best approach. This conversation must not be spread beyond these walls. I have not yet considered the implications. However far-reaching they are, they are serious."

"Of course, Lady Sage."

"And I will listen for any gossip that might arise. The Council is not nearly as circumspect as you, and there are too many who might have overheard their meetings." April twittered, not peeking up from her basket.

"Yes, do that, but be careful. This is dangerous ground." That was a dragon-sized understatement. "It would be useful to understand how far the information has spread. Still, it would take a great deal of temerity for a minor dragon to spread such gossip."

"Not as much as you might expect." Chisholm tucked her chin and whispered, as though uneasy about disagreeing. "Once word goes around, it is difficult to trace it to a source, and even the Council would be hesitant to take some sort of drastic action against many minor dragons."

"You make an excellent point, but it is a dangerous game." But then again, most draconic games were.

"I did not suggest that it was a good idea. But there are many frustrated minor dragons about who would like to see the Council and their ilk put in their place. And few would regret the loss of Cornwall."

"Has such a thing ever happened?" Elizabeth chewed her lower lip.

"If anyone knows, it is Drew—and since he always knows what is being said among the dragons, it is not as if you would be spreading gossip if you asked him."

DREW MET HER INSIDE the Library, only one floor below Elizabeth's quarters, so she was not quite breathless when she arrived. The door was still plain, an aching disappointment every time she encountered it. That her door should have been crafted before the Library's discomfited her soul, but if one considered the issues of dominance involved, it made sense in a uniquely draconic way. Even without a wonderful door, the Library stole her breath with the wonder of it each time she entered.

Its location at the end of the building allowed for high windows and reflecting mirrors on three of the four walls. The resulting bright light also rendered the room warmer than any other, drawing some to the Library and driving others away. April loved trips to the Library for just that reason. Today, though, she remained upstairs, tucked in her basket of warms.

Elizabeth sniffled away a sneeze and rubbed her nose with the back of her hand. It always took a few minutes to get accustomed to the scent of dust and books that went hand in hand with a collection this size. The smell of books, the smell of knowledge promising escape to faraway places and times, answers to burning questions, and sometimes more questions along the way, soothed her soul like nothing else.

"The information you are interested in is this way." Drew did not meet her gaze and kept his voice solemn. Clumps of dust clung to the edge of his dark-green head crest and a fine coat of dust blanketed his long snout. Neither of which was remarkable. If anything, such accessories were common for him.

But today, they were unsettling because she knew what he had been researching. Deep down, she had hoped he would find nothing and the Blue Order would be free of such intrigues as plagued warm-blooded society. But such naïve hopes were rarely rewarded.

They strode past rows of shelves, some with barely enough space to pass between. The end of each shelf had been carved with its own unique draconic patterns, some realistic, some resembling the creatures found in old manuscripts, drawn by scribes who obviously knew nothing about dragons. Shelves deemed to bear "important tomes" boasted marquetry, mosaic, and paint in their design. Humbler documents resided on shelves with modest—and sometimes difficult to tell apart—dragon scale patterns. On past forays into the library, the shelf-end displays had been amusing to study, but her mind was too full to consider the distraction today.

At the far end of the library, Drew turned down a narrow aisle, barely wide enough to accommodate a slender table that nearly blocked the passage beyond it. Three thick, dusty books—ancient, by the look of them—lay open along the table, butted up together as though to create some sort of continual narrative.

Elizabeth pointed to the books and cocked her head.

Drew nodded. "These are from a poorly recorded period of Blue Order history, during the reign of Edward II. These were not actually written during the early 1300s while he reigned, but a later retrospective, perhaps one hundred years later, maybe a bit more. Exact dates are difficult to discern."

"Can such a delayed account be relied upon?" Elizabeth pulled a small stool from under the table and eased herself onto it, her back brushing the shelves behind her. Heavens, it felt good to sit down.

"These were written by a dragon scribe, who I am reasonably certain saw the events firsthand, not second or thirdhand retellings." Drew stood on the opposite side of the table, fidgety paws resting on the table's edge.

"I do not doubt your expertise, but I am quite interested in how you can tell a warm-blooded scribe from a cold-blooded one?"

"Few have thought to ask that question." Drew brightened, the way he always did whenever his vast expertise was recognized. "It is not always easy. If you will permit me, I will show you what I consider to be incontrovertible evidence." He flipped the pages of the center book and pointed to an inkblot that covered several inches of the top corner of the page. "Examine that blot."

She leaned down and squinted at it. "Those look like scales! And is that a claw scrape?"

"Yes, indeed. I am certain of it."

"Forgive me, but I must ask. Are you certain it is a first-hand account by the scribe?"

"She notes it clearly. I have marked the pages." Drew touched several ribbons dangling at the top of the book. "Here, here and here, she notes in parenthetical text where her observations differ from the official accounts."

"Oh gracious, how did she ever slip in such information? Would not some supervisors have examined her work?" And how did he determine the scribe was female? She would have to ask him later.

"Scribes are far more clever than most people know." Drew edged in beside her. "Here, this is one of her parentheticals, directing the reader to the illuminations in the nearest margin." He rotated the book clockwise ninety degrees. "Look closely."

"Dragon script? Oh heavens, it is dragon script in the decorative patterns!" How many other books contained such documentation? Did anyone else know of these? Did Papa? How long had Drew been sitting with such information, not saying a word?

And how many other such secrets did he and others keep? Dragon's bones! She gripped the edge of the table and sucked in a deep breath.

"Can you read what it says?" he asked.

"I will have to rely upon your assistance. I am not yet satisfied with my fluency in the language." But that would have to change soon.

Drew's tail swung in a happy rhythm. "If you will allow me to take you through the narrative from the beginning." He pulled the first book closer. "I am certain you are well versed in the history of Edward II's reign, so I will not bore you with those details. What is less widely known, though, is that his approach to dragon Keeping alienated the Blue Order as much as his rule did the barons. The civil war of 1321 was as much a dragon uprising as it was a warm-blooded one. The human component of that war is fairly clear, but this is where it gets interesting."

He pointed to a passage in the first book. "You see here, the reference to a death at Painswick?"

"Yes, but I am not familiar with that name, either in the peerage or among dragon estates."

"That is by intention. At least that is what the scribe suggests. The death was of a dragon, one who vocally opposed both the king and the dragon he Kept."

"Was that Londinium?"

"No, it was not, and that makes it even more interesting. As I translate this, the dragon was a descendant of Britany. The Britany we read about in," he cleared his throat, "other documents. I am not entirely clear on that matter. The death at Painswick was under unusual circumstances. Suspicious circumstances."

"You believe it was not a natural death?"

"The scribe certainly did not, and at the moment, I have no evidence to disbelieve her."

Elizabeth refrained from suggesting that including hidden, unsanctioned messages might be a reason to do so.

"Here is where things get very interesting." Drew brought the second volume closer. "These passages, taken together with the marginalia, suggest a dark period among the dragons, when there was great division between those who followed Britany and those who followed another whose name is not given. The unnamed dragon, though, was a part of the Blue Order Council."

"Pendragon's bones!"

"Indeed, that dragon could have met Uther and even Dewi."

Elizabeth's face grew cold, and her skin twitched as though her scales had been rubbed the wrong direction.

"In the third volume, here, the death of Britany is noted, sometime during or after the reign of Henry IV. No description of that demise is included, beyond several repetitions of the note that the dragon died without reaching his full complement of years."

"Which you believe implied that Britany fell afoul of dark forces?"

"Given what I understand about Britany's rulership of the Order, I am uncertain I would consider those dark forces."

"Indeed? Tell me more."

"Britany was Brenin, both before and after Edward II. I should mention that not all those kings could hear dragons, which may well have been part of the problem with Britany, as major dragons without Keepers—well, perhaps I should not say, but the histories well document the issues."

Wait? Had he suggested there were monarchs who were not hearers? Was it not taught in the Order that all monarchs since Uther had heard dragons? One more thing she needed to discuss with Papa and Lady Astrid.

"In any case, Britany emulated Edward II in the way he played favorites and manipulated situations. Britany provided those favorites with greater territory and additions to their hoards. And suppressed the complaints of those, large and small, who suffered losses under his hand."

"That sounds like a dangerous game to play. Certainly, a dragon who rose to the rank of Brenin would have been—"

"One would think so, especially considering the wisdom Dewi passed down through the Blue Order about ruling those both greater and lesser in a territory."

Twice now he had referred to the 'lesser'. That could not be a coincidence. But what did he mean? Compared to a firedrake, who was not smaller and lesser in the kingdom?

"As there are terrible warm-blooded rulers, there is the occasional dragon leader who is less than optimal for the task. And by virtue of a firedrake's natural lifespan, they often rule much longer than warm-bloods." Drew's brow ridge rose, and he cast her a telling glance.

What was he trying to say without saying anything? She pressed her temples against a burgeoning headache. "Has any of Britany's line continued?"

"The current line of Brenin trace themselves back to Britany's dam rather than to Britany himself. She was Brenhines in the time of King Stephen and Matilda, which was in itself a period of great unrest."

"So, the line of descent is not straight."

"No, most definitely not. It was one of Britany's half-siblings, who took the name Londinium, and took over at his ... demise ..." Drew pushed the books back toward the middle of the table.

"And where do the current Londinium and Cornwall fit into the equation?"

"The Londinium of today is descended from that Londinium who was out of Britany's dam, and Cornwall is from Londinium out of the original Cornwall."

"It is possible, then, that Londinium had heard of the events you mention by firsthand account?" How mind-boggling that in firedrake lifetimes, the time of Edward II was just one generation ago!

"Possibly from someone who benefited." Drew turned his face aside as he said it. What was he watching for?

"Where could I find the records of the current Londinium's reign as Brenin?" Elizabeth pushed to her feet.

"I thought you might be interested in that." Drew beckoned her to follow as he trundled down the narrow aisle between shelves.

So he had expected that question, too? As clever as she had considered Drew before, she had underestimated him. Drastically.

He led her to a table on the other side of the Library, laden with open books, all old, but not nearly so old as the ones they had been reading on the other side of the Library. "Those are all the volumes on the current era of the Order. I have taken the liberty of leaving them open to what I expect will be the portions most interesting to you. I must now return to the Historian in the Archives. Pray, spend as much time with those volumes as you need." Another telling look. He dropped to all fours, touched his chin to the floor, and scurried off.

She brushed the dust off her sleeves, but the scratchy, irritable feeling along her arms remained long after the dust was gone. Settling on a convenient stool, she began at the leftmost book, which implied the starting place of another carefully constructed narrative.

Did she want Drew's interpretation, though? Clearly, he had an agenda of his own. Was that to be trusted? Until now, she had never doubted it.

Until now.

Perhaps she should start with what he had pointed out. Then, if it seemed too much, she could read the rest of the accounts. He had implied she would be welcome to take the books from the library to peruse at her leisure. More or less.

One issue at a time. She needed to focus. She forced her eyes to the first open page in the first book and skimmed through until she reached a carefully-placed ribbon. She had intended to pause and consider what she read after each book selection, but she tumbled into a story whose plot she liked less and less as she went on. Intrigues, deception, subterfuge, and a few hints of malicious harm, all pointing, more or less, directly to Londinium, often in the service of Cornwall.

What was that? A decree made by Londinium, two warm-blood generations past, saying something about minor dragons. But the full text had not been included, suggesting the proclamation was not a favorable one. Perhaps Papa had some access to the documentation. Drew probably did, but it would be better to hear it from Papa.

7
Chapter

ELIZABETH HARDLY SLEPT THAT night, between Baby Darcy's restlessness and her own restive spirit. At long last, the first rays of dawn broke through the darkness, giving her an excuse to stop tossing and turning, dress, and face the day.

"You are up quite early today." April twittered as she flew to perch on the bedpost nearest Elizabeth.

"Will it surprise you if I say there is a great deal on my mind?" Elizabeth rummaged through the press near the bed for clean body linen. Botheration—why was her bedroom always cold?

"Considering I am the one to blame for putting it there, no."

Elizabeth smoothed her dark blue skirt—that still smelled of dragon musk, like everything in the Order offices did—over her petticoat. She rubbed her tongue against the roof of her mouth.

Was it possible she could taste the musk, too? At least maybe now the chill would ease. "Is that what you meant when you said I might not like you telling me what you knew?"

"Not the only thing, but yes."

"What more do you know? Something about Londinium?" She sat on the edge of the bed to slip on her sturdy half boots, the most appropriate footwear to tackle the many staircases. Someday in the foreseeable future, she would need help to fasten her own shoes.

"His rule as Brenin has not been a good one. He cares only for himself and the most powerful in his domain."

"That seems to be a common malady among rulers."

April hopped to the bed beside her. "You will need to learn more about his reign. I lack the expertise to fully assist you with the matter."

"You have my word, I will. Before that, though, I need to learn more regarding Drew. Can you help me?"

"Your father's secretary?" April harrumphed, bright blue feather-scales fluffing. "He was an excellent choice for the position, as single-minded, stubborn, and irritating as our Historian."

"Stubborn and irritating?" Not words Elizabeth normally associated with the mild-mannered drake.

"He is as tight with information as the Council and unwilling to speculate on anything. So frustrating. He is not the one to turn to if one needs information quickly."

"Is that to say he is considered reliable, not trading in rumors and hearsay?"

"That is one way to put it. There are those who consider him eccentric, researching odd topics and ideas that others dismiss, especially as it concerns the oldest histories and documentation. He likes to find proof of his ideas before discussing them." April chittered under her breath.

"Is that a bad thing?"

"It depends on how much of a hurry one is in for the information. When he speaks, his ideas are interesting. But it takes so long for him to share them that few will bother asking him questions. He is so frustrating."

"Thank you. That is helpful."

"Did he tell you about one of his theories?" April hovered a hairsbreadth above the rumpled counterpane. "Oh, what did he say? Pray tell me!"

"He said nothing directly, so I cannot say just yet. I need to find out more, to be certain I understand."

April snorted with an ear-nipping look.

"Be patient. I do not want to give you misleading information."

"But you will tell me?"

"Of course, I will. You are my trustworthy Friend." She coaxed April to her finger and rubbed under April's chin and, if for only that tiny moment, the world became safe and normal again. "Have you any idea where Chisholm is?"

"Waiting for you in the parlor."

"Why did you not tell me?"

"Chisholm asked me not to wake you. She is quite content with her nose buried in that stack of books you had brought in from the Library."

"I suppose I cannot fault either of you for that." Elizabeth wrapped her blue woolen shawl around her shoulders and slipped into the parlor, April winging in ahead of her.

Two candles from an iron candelabra in the middle of the floor cast barely enough light to safely cross the room. Rosy rays of dawn struggled past frosted windows to paint the far wall in faint color. Only Chisholm, with her acute eyesight, could read under such conditions. She sat like a cat, with all four legs tucked up under her, an oblong, black dragonhide loaf, in the middle of a sea of books, with the room's sofa, chairs, and small tables pushed up against the walls to provide more space for reference material.

"Good morning," Elizabeth said softly.

Chisholm squawked and jumped, knocking several books aside. She landed on all four feet, eyes wide, panting. If she had been a cat, all her fur would have been standing on end and her tail pouffed. "Lady Sage!"

"Serves you right," April murmured as she landed on the mantel.

Elizabeth giggled and covered her mouth to contain it. "I am sorry. You must allow the humor of seeing you, of all creatures, startled and by me, no less."

"When you put it that way..." Chisholm snorted and shook her head.

"If it is of any consolation, I did not mean to surprise you. If anything, I was trying to avoid that very outcome."

"Of course, Lady Sage. Pray forgive my rudeness," Chisholm stretched out her front legs and touched her chin to the ground. "These manuscripts are so engrossing."

Elizabeth tapped the back of Chisholm's head. "I would very much like to hear your thoughts on what you have read."

"I have been concentrating on the most recent manuscripts, so I cannot comment on the matter of Britany yet." She glanced at the untouched pile of the oldest volumes stacked near the couch. "It may take me several days to fully grasp the volumes I am working on."

"Indeed? There is so much?"

"It is difficult to say precisely. There are many pieces, like an ancient mosaic, that I am trying to piece together. But I see several patterns of potential significance."

She forced herself to ask, "Pray tell me," though it was difficult to be certain she really wanted to know.

Chisholm pulled a padded footstool close to the books. "Perhaps you would be more comfortable sitting down."

So, this would be a long conversation. What that meant was challenging to predict. Elizabeth sat down.

Chisholm reached for a volume on the far left. "Are you familiar with the family lines of the English firedrakes?"

"I have a passing familiarity with them, but rely upon the records, should I need any details, which I confess I have never needed to pursue to date."

"Then I will simply summarize to say that with their long lifespans and sparse population, all the firedrakes are related more or less directly to the Brenin. Prior to the Accords, selecting the next Brenin had been a matter of dominance more than inheritance. The Accords attempted to designate it as a matter of inheritance to eliminate a motive for dragon war. Since they are effectively all related, the reigning dragon has selected the strongest firedrake, one expected to maintain dominance over the others, as the heir to take their place. The compromise allowed for the recognition of dominance that traditional contests would have observed, without the bloodshed that went along with it."

"And if there is opposition to the chosen successor?"

"It is dealt with before the need arises, in whatever way is most expedient in avoiding dragon war." Chisholm pushed the left-hand book away.

"There has not been a dragon war since the days of the Accords. That seems to imply the system works, yes?"

"The system has been untried. The first Londinium took the throne from Britany and, in time, it passed from him to the current Londinium. After the current Londinium reached his three-hundredth year, Cornwall was named heir and placed at Cornwall Keep. The way he managed his original territory marked him as the strongest of the firedrakes."

"Quite some time ago." It was tempting to ask how Cornwall had proven himself, but that would only distract. Elizabeth would examine the issue further on her own. When she had the stomach for the gruesome, bloody story it would likely be.

"Yes, it was. And yes, dominance patterns may have changed since that time. And no, there is no official mechanism to deal with that."

Elizabeth's skin prickled as she considered the implications.

Chisholm held her gaze for a moment, then turned back to another book. "That is not the only matter of interest. Some two hundred years ago, I cannot identify an exact date, but it was before Cornwall was installed at Cornwall Keep, there is a record of Londinium visiting Land's End, a visit that lasted several months. What happened during those months, well, I can find no record of it."

But a great deal could happen in that amount of time, could it not? Oh, heavens!

"After returning to London, Londinium began pushing for land enclosures, which most benefited the powerful firedrakes and their Keepers, and often subjected minor dragons to homelessness and hardship as they were forced off the lands they had occupied. The firedrakes and other large major dragons were only too happy to exercise their new form of dominance." Chisholm sat back on her haunches.

"Was Londinium aware of the consequences of his actions?"

"There is no direct record of that, but there are a few odd statements that suggest efforts were made to bring the matter to the Conclave."

"Who, of course, did not pay attention because it was not the major dragons who were affected." Elizabeth pressed the heels of her hands to her temples. "Did any of Londinium's other actions result in a detriment to minor dragons?"

"I do not know yet, but I can include that in my research."

"Do that. I somehow have a feeling that soon I will not have much time for digging through library volumes. Speaking of which, I suppose I should go attend to the Council now. They did not appreciate my begging off my meeting with them yesterday, and I have no wish to stir up their tempers."

APRIL PERCHED ON HER shoulder, twittering encouragement as Elizabeth trudged down multiple flights of stairs to the great courtroom and beyond to the Council's chambers. Was it possible the stairs grew longer and steeper, and the descent colder every time she attempted it?

Of course not. That had to be her imagination, but at the moment, she would have been willing to argue for the truth of it. She leaned back against the rough tunnel wall to catch her breath and gather her thoughts, neither of which proved easy.

A loud harrumph followed by a strong-smelling gust—dragon breath—poured through the open Council room door.

Duty called—or rather grumbled, whether her thoughts were in order or not.

Elizabeth pulled her shoulders back, straightened her spine, and walked through the doorway.

"Send the flutter-tuft away. We have no need of her." Cownt Matlock boomed from the far side of the room.

April squawked and zipped out the still-open door. Even she could not muster the courage to stand up to Matlock when he used such a tone. Exactly how far she might go and whether it would be out of range to eavesdrop, that was another matter entirely.

"She did not mean to offend, Cownt Matlock." Elizabeth curtsied, knee almost touching the floor. There was no need to increase his agitation. With any luck, she would be able to rise gracefully, though Baby Darcy's ill-timed kicking made it doubtful.

"Make certain she does not trespass again. Her kind is not welcome here." Cownt Matlock snorted. Dragon high dudgeon at its finest.

Barwin Dunbrook, his grey hide blending into the shadows, dull beside the two colorful dragons, stood to Cownt Matlock's right. The largest of the major drakes, he was larger than some firedrakes, and his pride was larger than that. To Matlock's left, Barwines Chudleigh, in her stunning jade green, winged and feathered glory, kept her head carefully lower than Matlock's, but even with Dunbrook's. The drake was the more massive dragon, but with winged flight to Chudleigh's advantage, it would have been a fairly even match between them.

Several torches lit the dragon-musky room, casting abstract shadows along the unfinished walls and floor. Odd that the Council would choose to meet in a chamber with so little grandeur.

"It was unwittingly done and will not happen again." Elizabeth struggled to rise from her curtsey. Odd, even Chudleigh glowered at her. "I am at your disposal. What did you wish to speak to me about?"

Dunbrook grumbled under his breath, as though she should be aware of such things simply because he did not want to be bothered to explain. "Have you met with the Historian?"

"Yes. As you requested."

"What news do you bring? What is that beaded nuisance you saddled us with up to?" Dunbrook's massive talons screeched against the stone floor, a sound surely intended to irritate her.

"Beaded nuisance? Do you mean Bede?"

"Who else?"

"If you find her problematic, I will reassign her elsewhere, far from these offices."

"Or I could simply eat her." Dunbrook bared his left fang in a sneer.

Elizabeth parked her hands on her hips and flared her elbows. If only she had thought to wear her cloak. "Barwin Dunbrook, are you implying a judicial action against Bede? Has she violated some edict of yours?"

"She is a nosy nuisance with a poor understanding of dominance and the tenacity of a tail mite."

Which was entirely true, but not illegal. "She irritates warm- and cold-blooded alike. But that is not a capital offense."

"It should be."

"If there is something specific—"

Matlock slapped his massive tail on the floor. The resounding thump pummeled her ears, almost louder than his growl. "She is not the issue we need to speak of."

"With respect, Cownt, I understand. But it seems there is a threat against her and since she was brought here under my dominance, I must deal with the challenge to my dominance first."

Dunbrook's eyes bulged, revealing a white ring along their edges. From the corner of Elizabeth's eye, Chudleigh seemed to turn her face away to hide a hint of satisfaction.

Matlock pulled himself up to his full height to tower over Dunbrook. "Dunbrook will not bother with her. Will he?"

Dunbrook's lip curled, and he snarled. "Tell her to stay away from the Council. I do not wish to encounter her in the halls, in the courtrooms, in the tunnels. If I cross paths with her again—"

"Understood." Elizabeth rapped her heel on the floor. Not a tail thump, but it would do. "If she bothers you again, her fate will be her own responsibility." What had Bede done to warrant such ire?

Dunbrook tossed his head and snorted.

"Enough." Matlock slapped his tail hard enough for Elizabeth to feel the jolt under her feet. "The matter at hand—"

"About the Historian." Chudleigh glided forward, her voice smooth, refined compared to the others. "You have met with him, yessss?"

"I have."

"And what did you learn?"

"In the interest of expediency, could you be very specific about what you are interested in? I cannot imagine the state of his aches and pains are of any interest to you."

"Not at all." Chudleigh's tongue flicked especially hard—a sign of irritation. "What of his research, of the archivessss? Of what Bede has been digging for?"

"Regarding his research, I do not think he has a great deal more to report. The translation process of dragon script is long and painstaking. As I understand, he has come to realize that there are many individual variations among the scribes, making it more difficult to be certain of any translation. He and Drew are trying to cross-reference each of their translations to be as clear as possible of their meanings."

"He has not told ussss of the issue." Chudleigh opened her iridescent wings and leaned toward Elizabeth, not quite treating her as prey. But it was certainly a warning—but of what?

"He and Drew and Quill Driver are only just now coming to grips with the magnitude of the discovery."

"It is a significant finding and has implicationssss for all the heretofore-translated documents?"

"Indeed, it does." Elizabeth met Chudleigh's challenging gaze. "They are so careful with their research and their conclusions. I expect they have not brought that to you yet because they are rechecking all their findings and making certain they only bring you accurate information, especially when it is so important."

"It reeks of trying to hide something." Dunbrook huffed a reeking breath in her direction.

"That is what the Hissstorian is supposed to do." The concession seemed to cost Chudleigh dearly.

Elizabeth coughed and swallowed back bile, pressing both hands to her belly as Baby Darcy objected. "Has that ever been his habit? Have you any evidence to suggest he is apt to do such things?"

"Everyone's agenda is suspect." Dunbrook snarled.

"That is enough." Matlock snapped his jaws in Dunbrook's face and turned back to Elizabeth. "Ensure that the Historian brings his conclusions regarding dragon script to us as soon as he is certain of the conclusions."

"Of course. That is his intention. I cannot predict how long that will take, though. There are a great number of documents to be analyzed."

Dunbrook's tail swept the floor, avoiding any contact with Matlock's tail. "And the Archives? What has he found in the Archives?"

"Do you mean the old room beyond the known Archives?" Gracious, she had to step carefully now. "There are many boxes and shelves to examine. He was clear that they had not even begun cataloging all the findings. As I understand, he is prioritizing the documents over the artifacts. I believe his strategy is to identify the nature of each document, sort and prioritize them, then work through to obtain complete translations."

"How long will that take?" Dunbrook said.

"Considering his suspicions about dragon script? I expect it will take years, unless there are more specialists assigned to his team."

"How many specialistsss on ancient dragon script are there in the Kingdom to assist him?"

"Therein lies the problem, Barwines."

"Has he any preliminary findingssss?"

"The concerns about dragon script are his preliminary findings. Beyond that, the records he has found are ancient and hard to read. Since there is so much ambiguity in the translation, he has made no definitive statements as to the contents of those records."

"And the itemssss they uncovered?"

"He has shown me nothing of those materials. He has deemed them of lesser value than the documents and is paying little attention to them."

"What is in those boxes?" Matlock boomed, his voice ringing like a gunshot from the surrounding stone.

Elizabeth fought not to cover her ears. "Is there something in particular you are interested in?"

"Find out the contents of those boxes."

"Shall I inform him of your interest in them?"

"No, there is no need for him to be aware of that."

"Then how am I to convince him to let me examine the materials?"

"That is not our problem." Dunbrook stopped short of snapping his jaws at her, nearly biting his tongue in the process.

No, she must not laugh. Such disrespect! What could be at the heart of it? "He will not permit me to poke around in his territory because I am curious. Would you allow another dragon to search your personal territory merely because they were interested in it?"

"He is a warm-blood, not a dragon." Dunbrook meant that as an insult.

"While that is true, you must understand, in certain in stances, we warm-bloods are every bit as territorial as any dragon, and do not tolerate violations of our dominance in our territory."

"Who is dominant, the Historian or the Scribe?"

"It depends upon the particular issue. They share dominance over the Archives and Library."

"Like a bonded pair?"

That was an interesting, if disturbing, comparison. "Their shared intellectual pursuits render them something of a bonded pair."

The dragons seemed to think about that for a moment.

"As Dragon Sage, your dominance supersedes—"

"With respect, Barwines Dunbrook, they will not recognize that. My territory as an officer is the relations between the warm- and cold-blooded. That has little to do with their Library or

Archives. When I use those resources, I do it under the auspices of their dominance."

Matlock slapped his tail against the wall. "You are being evasive and difficult."

"Hardly, Cownt. I am simply trying to explain to you the realities of warm-blood's territory and dominance, which is every bit as real, every bit as strong, as those issues among dragons."

"Are you refusing our orders?"

"I am making you aware of the problems with your demands. If you do not believe me, then by all means, remove me as Sage and find someone else who is better versed in these matters and can produce what you are asking for."

Matlock and Dunbrook growled, blowing fetid breath in her face.

"Stop!" She wrapped her arms around her belly. "There is no need to frighten the young one I carry. If you cannot control your tempers and treat me with the dignity of my office, I shall leave now. I will not tolerate this."

"It is as she says. The young one is distressed. This is no way for him to be introduced to dragonkind." Chudleigh spread her magnificent wings, blocking their view of Elizabeth. "Tell the Historian that I am trying to trace my line in England. Is there any evidence of amphithere artifacts in those archives?"

"Is that true?" Probably not the best response under the circumstances.

"From time to time, those who consider me an invader out of Sssscotland have challenged my right to hold my territory. It would be useful to be in possession of such confirmation to deal with those challengessss."

"He would be honored to help you establish your claim to your territory." In truth, that was exactly the sort of matter Papa would be honored to assist with.

"Offer to help him sift through the articles, then, and keep note of what you see," Matlock said.

"I will ensure you get an accurate inventory of the items, but I will do it as I see fit." Elizabeth looked Matlock directly in the eye.

Matlock stomped his forefoot. "You will—"

"Perform my duties in such a way as to offer the greatest likelihood of success."

"That issss the goal."

"Is there anything else? Or shall I get myself to the Archives now?" If only she could flair her hooded cape and stalk off in a display of "being big."

"There is one more thing," Dunbrook muttered.

She pulled back her shoulders and glared at Dunbrook.

"The beaded one. What has she been doing?"

"Only what the Historian has assigned her."

"And what is that?" Dunbrook spat the words, with a bit of spittle for emphasis.

"To discover what she can about the materials in the archive."

"What of her digging? What has she discovered?"

How much did Dunbrook already know? "She attempted to dig behind one of the bookcases, having heard that the wall behind it was hollow."

Dunbrook roared. "What has she found?"

Oh, now they had come to the real issue. "An area that was bricked over, intentionally sealed."

Dunbrook panted great gusts of fetid breath. "Is she still digging?"

"As I understand it, no, she is not."

"Then tell her, tell all of them, there is to be no more digging in the Archives. None." Matlock's voice dropped low and dangerous. A tone so reminiscent of Longbourn's treating her as prey that, had she had it on her person, she would have thrown down her badge of office and stomped out.

"I will convey the message."

"Do more than that. They must understand that any further digging, without express permission from the Council, from this point forward will be considered a capital offense. Judgment will be swift and merciless. Is that clear?"

"It is, Cownt." As clear as the point of his fangs, which he made certain to reveal. She drew a slow breath to quell the quiver in her throat. "I shall make it clear that there is to be no more digging in the Archives, effective immediately. Give me a way, a dye, a scent, something unique to the Council, something that can be obtained by no other means, and I will mark the limits of the digging that has already occurred so that there will be ready evidence if your orders are violated." Or if they have not.

"My venom, when dried, will create an orange mark which cannot be mistaken for any other ssssubstance." Chudleigh's head feathers bobbed as she cocked her head. "Will that do?"

"If Cownt Matlock will accept it, I will as well."

"Give her the venom."

8
Chapter

ELIZABETH RETURNED TO HER parlor to await the delivery of Chudleigh's venom. Amphithere poison was entirely different to a wyvern's, her sensitivity to which still kept her from visiting Longbourn for extended periods. So, Elizabeth should be able to handle it without harm. Or at least that was her working theory. If she were wrong, well, she would figure things out if it came to that.

Since amphithere venom was known for its healing properties, not its damaging ones, it would not likely come to that. Elizabeth was far more concerned with what might be important enough to drive Chudleigh to give it up. Amphitheres only produced minute quantities of that precious substance, and depleting their supply exhausted them, so no amphithere

offered it lightly. That Chudleigh did so now only emphasized the gravity of the situation in ways Elizabeth would
rather not consider.

How much should she reveal to Papa and Lady Astrid
about the matter? The Council dragons had not forbidden
it, so she would not be circumventing their demands if she
did. Not the way she had regarding the amount of digging
that Bede had done.

Technically, every word she had spoken was the truth.
That she did not offer a more complete explanation was
allowable under a strict interpretation of draconic rules of
conversation and negotiation. They had not asked a more
appropriate question, the sort they would have demanded
of an actual cold-blooded dragon. That was on them, not
her. She had conducted herself exactly as a dragon would,
exactly as she should have if she expected to be considered a
warm-blooded dragon.

But would that be enough to save her when they found
out, as they surely would? Would it be a situation of eat first,
ask questions later?

With some dragons it might well have been, but the
Council dragons were in their role precisely because of their
tendency to carefully consider actions and not behave with
typical draconic rashness. And eating warm-bloods was a
serious thing, especially if that warm-blood served as an
officer of the Order. That, of course, was not to say there
were no other means to remove troublesome officers. And
not all of those means included parliamentary proceedings.

She swallowed back the unpleasant taste in her throat and
soothed the hairs on the nape of her neck.

Merciful heavens! It hurt to consider dragons in that way.
But when one read enough of the histories, patterns became
obvious, obvious enough to serve as warnings.

Was that why Papa had been so insistent she read them, following her installation as Dragon Sage. Was he trying to warn

her without ever saying words that could put all of them in grave danger?

She had never thought of him as being so proactive, so devious—no, that was not the right word—so shrewd or calculating. Maybe that captured it more accurately. She would have to think on that more, when too many other heavy thoughts were not pressing on her mind.

What of Lady Astrid? Certainly, she was no naïve young woman. Considering the discreet stories she told of her late husband, she understood the world better than most. Did she see these matters for what they were? Did she recognize the threat she herself faced? Definitely time for a private conversation with Lady Astrid.

Elizabeth had come to London for intrigue, confusion, and strife. She had left Pemberley for safety, after it had been violated by the snapdragons, poachers and smugglers of dragons. But was this situation any better, with the sense of threat coming from the dragons themselves?

No. Not for her, not for her dragon companions, and most of all not for Baby Darcy, who seemed ever more restless, even troubled, with every new encounter or revelation. Perhaps it was time to declare enough was enough.

But was that the right decision? Though loath to admit it, and she would never say such a thing out loud, being with child had left her emotional, off-balance, not her usual clear-minded, rational self. Might her disquiet be the product of that?

If only she could talk to Darcy, listen to his opinions. He always helped her cut through the emotional fog—at least when she allowed him to. But letters would take days ... wait! Where was April?

Elizabeth hurried to her bedchamber and rattled the door of the wrought-iron fairy dragon 'cage' where April often retreated when she did not want to be bothered. April claimed to detect the noise from a great distance. Granted, it seemed fanciful, but it was better than simply waiting for April to return.

Elizabeth settled into her rocking chair. Perhaps it would soothe the baby, too.

A quarter of an hour later, April twittered in her ear. "I heard the rattle. Did you need me?"

Elizabeth jumped. "Forgive me, it seems I fell asleep while waiting. Yes, we must speak."

April cuddled into the side of her neck, her voice so low Elizabeth could barely make it out. "The rest of the Council meeting proved ... unexpected."

"I expect your thoughts are like mine?"

"Darkness in the coming days?"

"Yes. Darcy ..."

"And Walker, too. Brutus will find me an escort." She rubbed her head against Elizabeth's jaw and launched.

Elizabeth swallowed the ache in her throat. Such a dear little Friend, who knew her mind before she even spoke it. How long would April be gone, and how much longer would it feel? Elizabeth dragged her sleeve across her eyes and leaned into the down-filled rocker cushions. Baby Darcy liked this no better than she did.

An odd black shape slunk out of the shadows near the servants' door. Which dragon—no, it was two. Brutus strode forward with May clinging to his back.

"I will make the arrangements for April, Lady Sage." He stretched out his front paws, dropping his chin to the floor. May spring-hopped off his shoulders. "I know exactly the cockatrice for the job. Shall I alert Darcy House ..."

"Yes, tell them what you believe they need to know. Most of all, to be prepared." But for what? If only she herself knew.

"Immediately." Brutus dipped his head once more and disappeared into the service corridor.

May rose on her tail and put her paws up on Elizabeth's leg. Elizabeth patted her lap and leaned back to make room for the loudly purring tatzelwurm. The sound was second only to a fairy dragon's song in its soothing qualities.

"You both heard as well, then?" Elizabeth stroked May's soft fur. "You should not have been there. It is dangerous for you."

"It is dangerous for all of us. You can blame Brutus. He determined it necessary to observe. I followed to keep him out of trouble." May rose on her tail and rubbed the top of her head under Elizabeth's chin.

"So, you keep watch on him now?"

"When required." May leaned against her belly and purred louder.

"Is Little Anne as agitated as her ... brother ..."

"Yes, it is a male. April is not the only one who can smell it. And yes. Her naps have become fretful, and even dragon company does not settle her. There is unrest among all the minor dragons of the office. She feels it as much as you."

"Why has Mrs. Sharp not come to me with this? She knows I want to be made aware—"

"She regards it as merely the issues of teething, which she does not deem dangerous, as some do. Knowing you agree, she did not think it necessary to bring it to your attention, with so many other significant matters on your mind." May looked up at her with wide, golden eyes. "Mercy and Truth have done their best to keep the most unsettled minor dragons away, so Mrs. Sharp is not aware of the matters afoot."

"And you are making me aware of this now because..."

"You seem to have reached the same conclusion we have. Home is a good place to be."

Thanks to May's soothing purr, Elizabeth dozed in her rocker for the next quarter of an hour, images of Pemberley in her dreams.

A drake with a Blue Order livery badge woke her with a summons to Chudleigh's lair. Truth be told, despite its silk pillows and beautiful appointments, a dragon's lair was one of the last places she wanted to be. But no one expected Chudleigh to entrust her precious venom to any lesser creature. Only the Dragon Sage would be worthy.

But so many stairs! Who could blame her for taking her time getting there? No point in arriving breathless with heart pounding. Those were signs that prey displayed. Activating Chudleigh's base instincts would be stupid. And beneath the dignity of the Dragon Sage, something that bore remembering as well. The Council dragons had named her to the role. She ought to remind them of that lest they forget, as they seemed wont to do now.

Elizabeth's first view of Chudleigh's lair always proved startling. The space befitted a queen's dressing room far more than a dragon's lair. Almost perfectly round, the walls were lined with hollows filled with candles and mirrors providing enough light, not only to see the graceful swish of Chudleigh's lithe, bright-green, snake-type body against the pillows, but to read as well. Chudleigh did a great deal of reading.

And the pillows! Elizabeth knew no other dragon with a penchant for pillows like Chudleigh's. From her, Pemberley had learned to enjoy a pillow in her lair. A pillow. Not the three layers deep of down-filled cushions Chudleigh required. More fitting to a fine lady's boudoir, especially with the sweet floral notes that hung in the air. Amphitheres smelled like flowers. The gentle, feminine refinement of the space made it easy to forget a dragon resided here.

A major dragon.

A powerful, dangerous dragon.

"Barwines Chudleigh, may I enter?" Elizabeth called from the lair entrance, remaining just out of sight behind the final curve of the tunnel. With Chudleigh's recent pique, better to be cautious than bold. Providing venom would have exhausted her, and exhausted dragons were rarely gracious.

"I am expecting you." A low note in Chudleigh's voice suggested Elizabeth had made the right call.

Elizabeth entered slowly and struggled to lower herself into the proper arms-overhead-face-to-the-floor greeting.

"My venom is there." Chudleigh pointed with her tail to a glittering stoppered bottle on the shelf. "Apply it in the Archives immediately. Return the bottle to me when you finish. Do not hesitate. Treat it as a matter of life and death."

Elizabeth braced against the stone wall as she struggled to her feet. The faceted crystal bottle of bright-orange venom stood in a wall niche only a few steps away. "I will go directly to mark the extent of Bede's—"

"Vandalism."

"That is a strong word and implies at minimum mischief, or perhaps malice."

"That one is a dangeroussss dragon." The tip of Chudleigh's tail flicked. Her long, elegant multicolored head feathers bobbed in time.

"She is not even large for a minor drake. How can you consider her dangerous?"

"Her attitude, her ideassss. She does not understand the proper order of things, her proper place in the Order."

"And that makes her a threat?"

Chudleigh hissed a long sigh. "Not a threat, an irritation."

"Are you not above noticing small irritants?"

"She is not a small irritant. She is insidioussss."

"I do not understand what you mean by that." But Elizabeth definitely needed to.

"Her attitude is contagious, infectioussss. Other minor dragons are repeating her ideas, considering their worth, aspiring to leaving the sssphere to which they have been born." Chudleigh's wing flap stirred up the candle flames, dancing and flickering in the wing-wind.

Dragon's bones! She sounded like Lady Catherine and Rosings! "I have never experienced her expressing dangerous ideas. Irritating questions, yes. Demands for explanations of things which should need no explanation, yes. Failure to acknowledge precedence and dominance, yes. But those things are not what I consider dangerous."

"She questions the place of minor dragons in society. She questions the roles and rights of major dragonsssss. As though she and her kind have the strength to hold territory, much less manage it. It is not to be borne. She does not recognize the privilege she has to be admitted to these officessss, to the company of dragons far above herself. Now others are asking those same questions. There are far more important issues facing us. We do not have time for these irritationssss."

"You wish me to remove her—"

"I want her silenced, by whatever means necessary. Quickly, very quickly. If you do not manage it, then Dunbrook will. The next time she triessss to speak with us will be the last."

Elizabeth's heart clenched and somersaulted as images of Longbourn threatening her flashed in her mind's eye. "By your leave, I will go now and make arrangements." She backed towards the tunnel.

"And Lady Sage..." Chudleigh lowered her head to catch Elizabeth's gaze. "The way you stood up to Matlock and Dunbrook today, it was not lost on any of ussss. You might be considered among the major dragonssss of England, but that is a curse as much as a blessing. Every dragon knowssss there is a line which must not be crossed. Do not forget that."

"Yes, Barwines. Thank you for your concern."

"Go now. We will not ssspeak of this again."

Elizabeth curtsied and backed out of the lair.

What was she going to do with Bede? Was there any chance the persistent drake would listen to reason to save her own highly decorative hide?

9
Chapter

ELIZABETH HURRIED AWAY FROM Chudleigh's lair and head-
ed toward the Archives. Hurrying was more an attitude than an
activity these days, especially down the long tunnel to the deepest part of the Archives. Had she not needed to focus so hard on
careful steps and labored breaths, she might have contemplated
what she would say when she arrived. As it was, she paused at
the nondescript Archives door at the far side of the courtroom,
panting for breath, still wondering how to approach too many
delicate topics.

The door inched open, and Elizabeth gasped and jumped
back.

"Oh, pray excuse me, I did not mean to startle you, Lady
Sage." Quill Driver pressed the door open far enough to admit

her. "I heard someone at the door. Do come in." She jammed her key into the lock and turned it hard. A solid clank echoed off the stone walls.

Elizabeth pulled her skirts away just in time to prevent them from being caught in the door. "You seem anxious."

Quill Driver blinked and pushed her wire-rimmed glasses higher on her long grey nose. "Word travels fast is a common warm-blooded saying, is it not?"

No, no, no! It was never a favorable sign when dragons prevaricated. "Yes, I have heard that many times."

Quill Driver's brow ridge lifted, and she cocked her head as she took the single torch from the wall and silently led Elizabeth through the dimly lit rough room, filled with shelves and boxes, to the tunnel that led to the newfound rooms.

Light poured out from the end of the tunnel, enough for reading and study. Telling. Elizabeth followed Quill Driver in.

A small table and several stools had been added to the space, as well as three old wood and pewter candelabras that cast flickering light along the cave-like chamber. Lingering odors of old food and days-worn clothes mixed with the musty-dusty air. The overall effect did not improve the atmosphere.

Lady Astrid and Papa sat at the table, surrounded by scrolls and books. Was that a pallet in the far corner? Had someone been sleeping here? Lady Astrid would never consent to such a thing and the dragons eschewed such comforts. What could be so significant that Papa would sleep in the cold, damp chamber with nothing to soothe his relentless pains?

"You met with the Council?" Papa glanced up from the tome and adjusted his glasses. Pale, with dark circles under his eyes. How long had he been here?

Lady Astrid, who sat next to him, quickly looked up as well. Greying hair and dark-blue gown covered in a fine layer of dust, she looked no better than he.

"Yes." Elizabeth held up the crystal bottle of amphithere venom. "They have forbidden any further digging in the Archives.

I am sent to mark the limits of what has been dug so that any violations of their edict might be made plain."

"Is that amphithere venom?" Lady Astrid's jaw dropped, and she pushed to her feet.

"Chudleigh would never part with it for so ignoble a purpose." Papa sniffed and turned back to the nearest document.

"She would, and she did." Elizabeth dropped the bottle on the table with an echoing clink. "They are serious, Papa. There will be no negotiating with them. Pray do not make me force the issue."

"These matters are not their business!" Papa slapped the book in front of him. "They cannot interfere in my work as Historian!"

"I do not understand their reasons, but the Council does not act without purpose. I am sorry." Elizabeth pinched the bridge of her nose. "You must recognize, they are not aware of the extent of your discoveries or Bede's explorations. If they were to grasp the extent of those, I fear they would deny you access to the Archives altogether. I have done everything in my power to prevent that."

"This is unprecedented!" Lady Astrid gasped.

Papa's face turned a dangerous shade of puce. "I will protest—"

"It will be to no avail. Were you not listening? I have done everything I can to protect your access to what you have already discovered. Step aside and allow me to mark the current progress..."

Bede stuck her dirty snout out of the raw, recently-dug opening at the back of the room. "One moment more!" She disappeared into the shadows.

"No. I have already risked a great deal. You must stop immediately." Elizabeth picked her way across the rocky floor.

"Not to worry, I am done." Bede scurried past, dragging a small, dirty chest behind her.

"More?" Elizabeth choked out the words.

"It was hidden in an alcove in what seems to be a solid rock wall. I am certain I reached the limits of this chamber." Bede placed the trunk near the table. She was nothing if not persistent. "But there could be more. I am stealthy, I can—"

"No, Bede, you cannot. You cannot even continue to work here at the Order offices."

"She is my assistant!" Papa shouted. "You cannot simply march in here and take her from me. I—we—need her here."

Elizabeth grabbed the edge of the table and stood her ground. "You do not seem to be listening. It is not my choice, Papa."

"What do you mean?" Lady Astrid glanced from Elizabeth to Papa and back.

"The Council. I do not fully understand why, but they are stirred up to an extent I have never seen. I expect the issues with Cornwall and the dragon Sir Frederick encountered are largely responsible for the agitation. But there is more than that. The attitudes that are spreading among the minor dragons in the Order, for which they blame Bede, disturb them as well."

Bede worried her front paws together, dry scales scraping and rasping against each other. "Why blame me? I have done nothing wrong. Since when is it wrong to ask questions? I am only trying to understand."

"How many times must this conversation be repeated, Bede? I am not the only one who has explained the serious problems your relentless questions can cause." Elizabeth glowered, though Bede rarely responded to the expression.

"I meant no harm!"

"That may be the case, but what is done is done, and the Council dragons are troubled. I fear they have decided you are too much trouble to continue at the office. You are in grave danger."

"What does grave danger mean?" Bede cowered and edged back.

"Yes, Lizzy, what do they threaten?" Papa edged in front of Bede.

"Not to put too fine a point on the matter, I fear Bede's next encounter with any of them may be her last."

"They would imprison me?"

Now was not the time to mince words. "No, I think they intend to eat you."

Bede gasped and sat hard on her haunches. "Surely you must be wrong. I cannot be that bad."

"They are alarmingly agitated right now. At another time, they might not be so put out with you, but as it is, you are in immediate danger."

"I am sure if you let me talk to them—" Bede took several steps toward the door, but Quill Driver and Drew, who had appeared from the newest excavation, blocked her way.

"No." Quill Driver barked like the large dog she persuaded the dragon-deaf she was. "If Lady Sage says you are in grave danger, then it is so."

"There is a reason she is Sage. You must believe her." Drew chittered something sounding much like dragon-tongue.

Quill Driver and Bede gasped, jaws dropping. What had he said?

"What am I to do? Where am I to go?" Bede asked, looking from one warm-blood to the next.

"I am considering several possibilities. Give me a few days to work it out. I will find a solution for you. I just do not know what that looks like yet."

Papa patted Bede's shoulder. "You must protect her. Bede is necessary to our efforts here, endeavors that are too important to abandon."

"He is right." Lady Astrid stood next to Bede. "Only yesterday we translated another section in the saga of Uther and Dewi and ... well, if the Council is agitated now, this will not improve matters."

"What did it say?" Elizabeth clutched her forehead with one hand and pressed her restless belly with the other.

"I will read it!" Bede scurried to an open volume on a stack of boxes.

I had hoped never to write these words, but if things continue unchanged, it may be the only record of major dragons in this land. So, I, Scrivener the Lesser, by Scrivener the Younger, out of Whiptail the Intrepid...

Bede glanced over her shoulder at them. "I will skip the rest of the genealogy, which goes on for five more generations. You, of course, may examine it if you wish to study that aspect further."

"Pray go on," Elizabeth summoned every ounce of control not to yank the document out of Bede's claws. Not that it would help, especially since Elizabeth's grasp of ancient dragon script was rather wanting.

"As you wish."

So, I, Scrivener the lesser out of and by many generations, leave this record of what might be the last battle of the dragon wars.

Elizabeth pulled out a stool and sat down hard. Final battle? How could that be...

Britany and those who followed him attacked the warm-blood contingent, certain of their victory, but their hubris has been their downfall. The warm-bloods ringed their camp with fires to which they fed articles—which for self-preservation and the preservation of all who might survive to read this, I shall not name—creating a smoke that while unpleasant to the warm-bloods was a pernicious toxin to the firedrakes. They dropped one by one from the sky, where they succumbed to the iron weapons of the warm-bloods.

Britany, the strongest of them, made it back to dragon-held territory, but his injuries will leave him unable to exert his dominance for quite some time, rendering the remaining firedrakes without a dominant dragon. Chaos will ensue, and the species might be lost forever.

"Merciful heavens!" Elizabeth pressed her fist to her mouth. "Is that possible?"

"There is no reason to think the scribe invented such a tale. How dangerous would it be for a minor dragon to say such things about firedrakes if they were untrue?" Papa harrumphed and perched on a stool near Lady Astrid.

Dewi and his followers did not take part in Britany's ill-fated raid, but Dewi's coalition is now fractured and in danger of dissolving, which will hardly improve the situation. Dewi himself questions the expediency of a treaty with the warm-bloods now they have found an effective weapon against his kind, and the peace talks I hoped and advocated for may never come to pass.

I might be only a minor drake, from a minor line of drakes in service to the firedrakes, but I must do my duty. There is only one choice; though it may cost me my life, I will do it.

I must, somehow, convince Dewi and the warm-bloods' leader, whom I have heard called Uther, to enter discussions for peace.

"I do not imagine the Council will like that much, will they?" Bede sat back on her haunches, a self-satisfied smile lighting her face.

"I do not imagine that they will." Lady Astrid removed her glasses and polished them with her sleeve. "The knowledge that there was some warm-blood weapon used effectively against firedrakes—I cannot fathom their reaction."

"I can." Papa frowned with his whole body. "It will not be pleasant or in any way moderated. They have been comfortable with their near-invincibility for generations. To lose that now, as so many other things are changing around them, could be devastating."

"But there was no explanation of what the poison was. That is important, no?" Quill Driver shrank back as she spoke.

"It does not matter," Papa said. "Simply exposing the fact that there is such a thing, and the mode by which it was delivered, means that it is only a matter of time before someone discovers the identity of the substance."

Elizabeth squeezed her eyes shut and shook her head. "I am not sure that is the worst of it. Given their alarm with Bede and the questions she is causing other minor dragons to ask ... This document implies that the minor dragons played a foundational role in the Pendragon Treaty and Accords. Tradition teaches that the major dragons, and in particular the firedrakes, are responsible for the treaty, and are owed gratitude for the action, especially since it gave favor and precedence to the warm-bloods, who did not deserve it, and conceded the right to exist to minor dragons, who were barely above prey."

"Dragon's blood!" Lady Astrid spoke through her hand tightly pressed to her mouth. "You are correct. This could turn around almost every assumption we hold about the Accords."

"And the Council will not like it." The words fell from Papa's lips like an executioner's axe.

10
Chapter

"Thank you for coming to meet with me." Elizabeth ushered Wentworth into her office, where a cheerful fire and a simple breakfast of tea and buns waited well away from the growing pile of books and other work on the mammoth desk. Leave it to Chisholm to stay abreast of such niceties when the weight on Elizabeth's mind drove out everything else. "I know you are busy preparing for your trip to Land's End."

Sir Frederick chuckled as he followed Elizabeth to the comfortable leather wing chairs near the glowing fireplace. His quiet self-assurance offered a gentle balm to her tension. "Be that as it may, one does not refuse an invitation from the Dragon Sage."

"I am not sure how to take that. One does not ignore a ranking dragon's summons, but—"

"Are you not considered among the ranking dragons? Order members are encouraged to believe so." He cocked his head and raised an eyebrow.

"It is a hard distinction to bear. And an honor I am not quite certain how to reckon. Please, sit down."

"Forgive my jest. I did not mean to cause you discomfort. I am honored by your consideration." His awkward expression suggested he was still working out the rules of the strange social order of draconic society.

"Now that we have both been most polite and proper, perhaps we can actually enjoy a conversation."

"Indeed." He settled into his seat, face turning somber. "May I inquire why you suggested that Laconia not join us today? As it is, he had other matters to attend to, but it seems out of character for you. To be honest, he might have been offended, though he never came out and said so directly."

"It is unusual, and I hated to exclude him. But there is something I must ask of you that is of a sensitive nature that I thought would be better expressed in privacy." Elizabeth poured tea for them both and offered him a plate.

He glanced around the room as he reached for a sweet bun. "No offense, Lady Elizabeth, but are you certain of our privacy?"

"Chisholm has assured me our conversation is private. She and Brutus are patrolling the tunnels and back corridors to ensure that it remains so. May is making similar patrols."

"What matter requires that level of confidentiality?" He set his plate aside and leaned forward, elbows on his knees.

She wrapped her hands around her warm, fragrant teacup and stared into it as a stray tea leaf swirled about the bottom. "I have a difficult, and even dangerous, favor to ask of you."

"What matter involving dragons is not dangerous? I am at the service of the Blue Order."

"I count on that." She looked up, met his gaze, and held it. He did not waver or hesitate. "Where to begin? Have you made

Bede's acquaintance? She is one of the Historian's assistant drakes."

"I do not believe so, but Laconia has mentioned the name once or twice. Not in complimentary ways, if I recall correctly."

"I am not surprised. He is such a sensible fellow." Elizabeth forced herself to sip her tea. Perhaps that would settle her stomach. "Bede spends most of her time with my father researching ancient documents and seems to share several of his less agreeable traits."

"Is she a black and white speckled drake? Laconia mentioned an interesting conversation with a drake of that description."

Dragon's fire! "Did he mention the topic of their exchange?"

"No, I do not recall that he did. But afterwards, he expressed a newfound respect for her despite her less admirable qualities." Wentworth tapped steepled fingers.

"It is fortunate she has not alienated Laconia as well. That would render things more difficult than they already are."

"Is Bede in some kind of trouble?" Wentworth took a bite of his Chelsea bun, chewing slowly, thoughtfully.

"As a matter of fact, yes. In short, Bede has attracted the Council dragon's attention, and not in a favorable way."

"I doubt there is a favorable way a minor dragon might come to the attention of the Council, eh?" He chuckled a dark, gallows note. "I expect the problem is serious?"

Elizabeth set her teacup aside and folded her hands in her lap. "It would not be going too far to assume that her next encounter with any of the Council will be her last."

Sir Frederick straightened abruptly, his expression saying everything. "What help do you need?"

Elizabeth's held breath rushed from her lungs, and she nearly sagged as the pressure left her chest. "She must be removed from the Order offices, from London. You will travel soon, no?"

"I expect orders directing Laconia and me to Land's End at any time."

"And Laconia is not hostile toward Bede?"

"Not to my knowledge, but I must ask, why not inquire of Laconia himself?"

Elizabeth leaned her head back and stared at the cobwebs in the ceiling's corner. "I respect Laconia a great deal and admire his loyalty to the Order. I am concerned that if I asked him directly, he might not be as honest as I would prefer."

"He is as direct as any dragon. I am surprised it would be a concern to you."

"I do not doubt it. But—" Dragon's bones! How much should she say?

"You are afraid something would override his natural forthright tendency?" He rubbed his knuckles along his stubbled jaw. "That is worrisome."

She nodded with a small frown. Pray he did not press—

"Might that have something to do with the current mood among—"

"Yes, quite." Even in privacy, some things did not need to be spoken aloud.

"I am afraid I still do not understand. If he would be willing, despite his preferences otherwise, why would it be a problem? I am not sure why you cannot order her to safety. The minor dragons revere you so—"

She sighed. If Sir Frederick had ever met Bede, he would never ask such a question. "Given her peculiar nature, I cannot demand she do anything and expect it will happen. She requires a close watch as she is escorted to a new assignment. An extremely close watch. She is well-meaning, to be sure, but distractible, and not apt to grasp what is intuitively obvious to others. She needs a purpose, a challenge, to keep her focused away from dangerous diversions."

"I imagine, then, as you are implying you wish to send her with me, you expect reestablishing a proper regional office in Lyme might be an acceptable option? Certainly, you cannot be contemplating sending her to Land's End and Cornwall."

"Oh, heavens, not that!" She laughed and shuddered at the same time. Cornwall would bring a quicker end to Bede than Dunbrook! "I was definitely thinking of Lyme. Mr. Wynn is serving as a temporary Blue Order magistrate there, is he not?"

Sir Frederick snorted and shook his head. "Yes, but to be honest with you, most find him abrasive, judgmental, and challenging to get along with. I am not sure—"

Of course he was. Elizabeth joined his headshaking as she laughed—not the happy manner of laughter, but the sort that bubbled out when there was no other expression possible. "Actually, all things considered, that is a good thing. Bede is difficult to get along with. But she and my father, whom many regard as rather troublesome, maintain an adequate working relationship. It is not beyond imagination that she may suit Mr. Wynn well."

"He is the kind of man who seems to prefer draconic company to warm-blooded companionship. So it could work out. He has his hands full right now, as they discovered boxes and boxes of records and books and whatnot that Allenden ignored during his tenure. A common practice of the past magistrates at Lyme as a whole. As I understand, none of them—for a long time, at least—have been Keepers and, as such, their commitment to the Order was on the lax side."

"I am afraid that tendency turns up more often throughout the Order than any of us would prefer." She pressed her temples. "That makes Bede, for all her challenges, extremely important—she has unique skills which the Order, whether or not they acknowledge it, cannot afford to lose. So, it is imperative I find the right situation for her."

Sir Frederick stroked his chin. "Anne might help as well. She is the soul of patience toward difficult personalities, warm- or cold-blooded."

"Between her father and Kellynch, she must be."

"Have you met her Friend Balen? She has been to London several times, delivering messages for us. Theirs is a recent

Friendship, but one I am quite certain will stand the test of time."

"Yes, Balen is a fine, stable Friend. April respects her, which says a great deal. If Balen is willing, she would probably be an excellent influence on Bede, as well." Elizabeth tried another sip of her tea. That helped settle her stomach a mite. "I confess, that is part of the reason I thought to approach you. Kellynch-by-the-Sea seems to be uniquely qualified to manage a very sensitive situation."

"And by that, you mean we are far from London and the estates of any of the Council dragons?"

"Both are admirable qualities, though not the only ones I was considering. Are you willing to take on such a responsibility, understanding how much rides upon your success?"

"I am not sure I understand that." Sir Frederick scratched the back of his head. "But that has ever been the case in my naval career, so it is nothing new. I do not prefer to speak for Anne, but in this case, there seems little choice. I will take Bede to Lyme and see that she is properly supervised."

"Excellent. When shall you leave?"

"Not for several days at least, even after my orders arrive. It seems there are more preparations than I expected for my journey. As I understand, Buckingham—or is it Londinium? I forget which to use—desires to send a private message to Cornwall, and it is taking some time to craft the missive and then have a scribe put it to paper according to all the proper forms and conventions."

"And there are many of those, to be sure." What could Londinium need to say to Cornwall via an official messenger? Whatever it was, it did not sound positive. "How long do you suppose it will take?"

"Honestly, I have no idea what to expect. I am a naval captain, not a messenger. How urgent is the errand?"

"If Bede is talking to other minor dragons—and what you said regarding Laconia implies she is—then I would prefer not

to wait another hour to remove her from these premises."
Yesterday would have been better, but if wishes were horses,
beggars would ride—and maybe tatzelwurms would fly.

"Unfortunately, I am staying in quarters upstairs, which
affords me no sanctuary to offer her in the meantime."

"Oh, there is a thought." Elizabeth drummed her lips with
her fingertips. "Perhaps I can send her to Darcy House. Slate
and Amber are quite adept at managing guests, as are their
Friends, Mr. and Mrs. Davies, our butler and housekeeper.
I should assign Axel to help as well. Slate and Amber are all
kindness and courtesy. They will need Axel's growl and teeth
to support their efforts."

"I have found that a sound system for dealing with re-
calcitrant sailors." He laced his hands behind his neck and
stared at the ceiling. "May I ask a personal question?"

"After all that I am asking of you, you are due that."

"The threat to Bede that you just described is … 'serious'
would be an understatement. Does it make you uncomfortable, or has such a thing become normal to you as often as
you deal with dragons?"

Her stomach clenched into a Gordian knot. "You are experiencing discomfort after the battle in Lyme Bay, or with
your encounter with Chesil?"

"Both." He glanced away. "Not to be too personal, but I
find I often relive both those experiences in my dreams, and
it is not pleasant. Is that phenomenon … I cannot use the
word 'normal' to describe anything related to dragons, so
perhaps 'typical' might better capture my question."

No, there was absolutely nothing normal about living with
dragons. "I hesitate to speculate on what might be typical in
these circumstances. There are so few of us who have survived
such encounters, and far fewer who have left some sort of
records of them, that there is little to draw from." She turned
aside to stare at the wall opposite to the one he stared at. "That

is why I asked you to record your experience, even to the point of including such personal details."

"What of your experience, though?"

"I still have disturbing dreams. Occasionally, those feelings will intrude on my waking state, when there are reminders of the encounter, like a smell, or visiting the place it occurred. Even encountering that same dragon type can be uncomfortable." Very uncomfortable, even with pleasant ones like Uppercross. She gripped her upper arms, the pressure dispelling some of the urge to flee.

"I see. So I should not be concerned that I am..."

"Losing your mind?"

He guffawed. "Yes, that."

"No, not at all. There is a tendency, perpetuated by the Order itself, to downplay such encounters and suggest that the warm-blooded reaction to them is excessive."

"What do you think?"

An all-too-bitter laugh escaped. "Having been in the talons of a dragon whom I once considered friendly and reasonable, poison breathed in my face, his teeth inches from my person, and no certainty as to his true intentions, I would say no, it is not excessive. When one fears for their life, who is to say a reaction is excessive?"

"The dragons, I suppose." He shrugged, staring at the floor.

"I have been told that in their view, the problem is the warm-blood perception of threat." She reached for another sip of tea. "Those same voices have also said that it is clear in the details of the situation that no actual threat to life and limb was present. We warm-bloods are at fault for misreading the event and any troublesome effects we experience result from our deficiencies alone."

"Convenient, that, no?" He clucked his tongue. "What would those clear details be, in precise terms? It seems important to understand."

"That we survived, Sir Frederick, that we survived is the sign." She pinched her temples with thumb and forefinger, closing her eyes.

"Not wholly satisfying, is it?" He leaned against the back of his chair. "Are there many records of those who did not survive?"

"Since the signing of the Accords, the only known records of dragon aggression against warm-bloods relate dragons lashing out in self-defense."

"That did not apply in either of our cases, did it?"

"No." Did Baby Darcy not like her answer, or did he dislike the whole conversation altogether? The way he kicked, it was difficult to tell. She ran her hands along her stomach.

"How do you do it, then? Continue to face the dragons that could turn on you in an instant, day in and day out, knowing they would meet no consequences for their actions?"

"I try to think like a dragon and act accordingly." She pressed her palms to her belly. "But it is not easy. Especially now, it is not easy."

"Would it be different—would a dragon like Cornwall treat you differently—if you had a more powerful dragon, a fully-grown one, in your Keep?"

"It is hard to say. It makes sense it might deter some, but I was Keeper to Longbourn when he acted badly, so the question does not apply in that situation."

"Forgive me if I have stirred up an uncomfortable topic. I had no intention of doing so."

"Sometimes life is uncomfortable, and it is better to face it head-on than to let it attack you from behind, no?"

"That sounds like something a dragon would say."

A quarter of an hour later, Sir Frederick left, promising to send word to Lyme of their plans, and to work with Chisholm that very afternoon to compose the records Elizabeth had requested.

After seeing him to the door, Elizabeth sank down in the dark-blue wing chair and held her shoulders tight. Even now, she avoided thinking about Longbourn. Despite his draconic, unsatisfying apology, things had never been the same. They never would be. Yes, she had the excuse of extreme sensitivity to wyvern venom, and while that was true, it was hardly the only reason she had not visited Mary and Mr. Collins and Longbourn, and she avoided calling upon Longbourn when he came for the Dragon Conclave.

The sight of him still left her looking for the nearest escape, while her body prepared to flee at the first twitch of a wing. Only April, Darcy, and Walker knew the truth. She had never told Longbourn; he might have suspected, but said nothing. If he had changed his behavior because of it, she had never given him the chance to demonstrate it.

And probably never would.

Perhaps she should tell him. But even if it did not raise his ire, it risked his turning the blame onto her and her warm-blood weakness. Not something she was ready to ask for. Not yet. Maybe not ever.

Was that cowardly?

A shadow moved in the dragon tunnel entrance in the corner next to the fireplace.

Chisholm.

"Lady Sage?" The secretary drake touched her chin to the floor.

"Yes, do come in." Elizabeth righted her posture and tried to arrange her expression into something more dignified.

"I imagine you have additional tasks pursuant to your meeting?"

"I imagine you heard a great deal of that encounter." Elizabeth let her raised eyebrow ask the question.

"You did request that I patrol the tunnels to ensure that you were not otherwise overheard. I had no intention of eavesdropping."

"Of course, if you were there, you could not help but hear." Elizabeth held her breath lest she sigh.

"You know that I will hold my peace."

"I have no choice but to believe that. Forgive me, that was ungracious. I find myself rather taxed." She pressed her cool palm to her forehead.

"Of course. Shall I call for more tea?"

"And a bit of dry toast, if you will. A touch of indigestion has accompanied this meeting."

"Shall I do that now, or is there other business?"

"Tea and toast are definitely not the most pressing thing on my mind, no. And I am sure you have already anticipated my next question."

Chisholm sat back on her haunches and worried her front paws together. "Regarding Bede?"

"Has she been talking to the other minor dragons in the office? Or, perhaps more accurately, what has she been saying to them? I expect she has not curbed her tongue."

"You are correct; she has not." Chisholm looked down, shrinking in the face of the more dominant dragon.

"I do not, and will not, hold you responsible for delivering news that I dislike. After all, I asked you to tell me."

"Of course, Lady Sage." Chisholm inched back. "Most of the office staff dragons avoid her. They find her as tedious as the dragons at Pemberley did. However, there are certain topics which inspire others to listen to her."

"And those topics are?"

Chisholm shuffled her feet "Related to defying, or at least irritating, the Council dragons."

Elizabeth slapped her forehead. "Is that to say Bede has been intentionally working to provoke their ire?"

"No, that is perhaps the most vexing thing. She does not seem to understand why the Council dragons are irritated by her efforts. Nor does she seem to comprehend why the other minor dragons listen to her when she speaks of those things.

But, as I have heard, Bede is quite pleased to be taken seriously by the others, even if she does not fathom why."

The worst possible combination. "Then there is no time to waste. Tea and toast will wait. Call Brutus and Axel in to see me and find Bede and bring her here directly. Do not tell her to come, but bring her here yourself. There must be no delay, no distraction. From here on out, she cannot leave our supervision."

"As you say, Lady Sage." Chisholm bowed, chin to the ground, only the stiffness of her movement giving away her feelings on the matter.

Though she dare not declare it aloud, Elizabeth could hardly disagree.

11
Chapter

SLEEP FOUGHT HER THAT night, like a swarm of angry forest wyrms, at last bringing dreams of impassioned dragons that left her breathless and flailing as she awoke. There was a reason she did not talk about Longbourn easily or lightly. The day the dragon she Kept had turned on her had changed her in ways she still could not fully name. And brought on dreams to prolong the torment. Not that the Council's churlishness did anything to ease her dark thoughts...

She hauled herself out of bed—had she increased so rapidly with Anne? She did not remember it that way, but it was not as if she kept a record of those details in her commonplace book. It had not stood out as important to keep track of at the time. She tied her dressing gown around her bulging waist and paced.

Unfortunately, pacing the floor only aggravated her aching back and triggered those nagging pains that reminded her that travail was only a few short months away. Merciful heavens, birth had been hard with Little Anne. She shivered at the panic that hovered at the edge of her awareness.

Mama had promised her that those memories would fade in the delight of a newborn. She had only been half right. Little Anne was a delight, but those memories—they joined with those of Longbourn and Cornwall, haunting her sleep, and occasionally her waking moments.

Did she really want to give birth in London? It had seemed a good idea when she and Little Anne had left Pemberley. But with the Council so agitated and the minor dragons unsettled, would she be able to rest and attend to their new little one, the son that April insisted it would be?

Assuming, of course, she survived the ordeal.

Dragons, on the whole, had scant compassion for the process of pregnancy and childbirth. Laying eggs was a natural and not terribly uncomfortable process. While Cait had suffered through complications, those were rare, and considered part of the natural order of things. If those who experienced them died, well, it was better that the weak did not reproduce.

Which explained Cait's undraconic gratitude for Elizabeth's help in surviving the experience.

She shook the weight of the memory form her shoulders. Draconic 'compassion' was most definitely not the attitude she wanted in a midwife. Travail with Anne had been long and hard and she had required every day of the six weeks of her lying-in to recover from the experience. To survive that, she had needed the sort of compassion that was the purview of warm-bloods.

Elizabeth leaned against the wall, hugging her shoulders, and swallowed back the bitterness on her tongue. The midwife had assured her that the problems associated with Anne's birth were most likely related to Anne's great size, her odd position, and a few other issues that were specific to Anne herself. Not likely to recur in another childbirth.

Not likely.

Not likely did not mean impossible.

Everything that had been unlikely with Anne could happen again.

Dread she could not voice wrapped stiff fingers around her throat. Suffocating. Her heart beat harder, trying to drive it back. It was not as though there was no one who could understand. Lady Dressler, Aunt Gardiner … yes, they would understand. But to actually speak the words risked that they would be overheard and her weakness would become known among the dragons.

How would that affect her role as Sage? Possibly not at all. She was warm-blooded, after all, and subject to those foibles, just as the cold-blooded were to theirs. But to run that risk now, with the Council so agitated—no, she could not take that chance.

She held her stomach with one hand and eased herself into the rocking chair. Mrs. Sharp said that it was not healthy for her to dwell on uncomfortable things. The fretting would change nothing.

Which was entirely correct, but those thoughts could help her plan for the future. For one thing, her will had been written in anticipation of Anne's birth and would need to be changed. She needed to ask Chisholm's assistance with that.

If the worst were to happen and she and the baby were lost—she squeezed her eyes shut and held her breath; crying would not improve matters. She pressed her fist to her mouth and bit her knuckle. Yes, tears might relieve her at the moment, but they would change nothing.

If things went badly, what then? With only her father here in London, who would make certain that her wishes would be carried out? Would Chisholm be permitted to manage her affairs, or would she be immediately reassigned to other duties? Were

Mrs. Sharp or Mr. and Mrs. Davies at Darcy House equipped for the task?

And if the baby survived without her, then would Mrs. Sharp be able to get both children back to Pemberley? Would Allister Salt be available to take them, or would his services end with her last breath? No doubt Aunt Gardiner would help ...

And what of Darcy?

No doubt the blow would be hard on him. Devastating, even. But to hear it from a messenger or in a letter sealed with black wax? Nausea rose. She covered her mouth with her hand. No, she could not do that to him. He deserved better than that.

Whatever happened, they would face it together, as they had with Anne.

She had to return to Pemberley.

She should never have come to London. But the pregnancy was barely a reality then—Matlock had blurted it out in the most draconic way, for his purposes, heedless of any warm-blooded courtesy. If she thought about it, she had felt Baby Darcy moving by that point. But there was so much else happening, she had dismissed it all as indigestion. She should have been more attentive to the signs and what they might mean.

But after what had happened with Anne, she could hardly bear to reflect on such things, especially when the threat from the poachers and smugglers had been so close and so real. Coming to London had made a great deal of sense.

In that moment, it made sense.

But now everything was different.

The threats from Cornwall and Chesil superseded all else. But there were other important matters demanding her attention. In some ways, the Council's single-mindedness seemed rational, but to ignore internal issues in favor of those other matters seemed short-sighted at best.

The baby kicked her rib, and she pressed that spot hard. Oh, that was another disturbing thought. If they were so concerned with Chesil, why would they also be worried about Papa and Bede? That did not seem consistent …

unless…

Unless they had some inkling of what Bede might find, and viewed it as threatening to them as an enormous sea dragon threatening the heir to the Blue Order throne.

"Lady Elizabeth?" Mrs. Sharp touched Elizabeth's shoulder. "Is something wrong?"

Elizabeth jumped and shook her head, dislodging the sleep from her mind and clearing her bleary eyes. When had she settled into her rocker? Was it a bad sign she did not remember walking into the parlor in the first place? Had the fire been lit in the room when she sat down? No, one of the staff must have lit it while she slept, long enough ago that its warmth had forced the cold back towards the window and exterior wall, to be mellowed by the morning sun.

May purred in her lap, kneading her leg like a kitten. When had the tatzelwurmling joined her? "No, just uncomfortable last night. I suppose I fell asleep in my chair."

Mrs. Sharp stroked her cleft chin, her bright-green eyes narrowing. "It is hard to work out how that rocker might be more comfortable than your bed. Perhaps a fainting couch might be acquired for you. It would provide the advantages of both the bed and the chair. I am sure I can arrange for it to be done today, tomorrow at the latest."

"About that, though…"

"Is there some other room in which you would be more comfortable? Would you prefer to remove to Darcy House?" Mrs. Sharp's brows rose high on her forehead. "That is, of course, possible, and it might do you well to be away from the strain and constant demands of the Order offices. I fear the daily walk to and fro will only grow more uncomfortable as time progresses, though. How swollen your ankles have become in the last week or so! So perhaps a sedan chair might be in order?"

"Really?" Elizabeth stared at her feet. Gracious! "I had not even noticed that. But you are correct. I am growing more and more restive here and am considering—"

"Removing to Pemberley?" Mrs. Sharp whispered.

"Yes, that was the thought."

"You should do that." May rose on her tail and looked Elizabeth in the eye, purring louder. "That is an excellent idea." May's tone was the same one April used when she was disturbed or frightened.

"Why do you say that?" Elizabeth stroked May's pouffed fur.

"I am sorry, Lady Sage, I should not have—" May put her paw on Elizabeth's shoulder but turned her face aside.

Elizabeth tipped May's chin so their eyes met. "Yes, you should. I have always told you to bring any concerns you have to me without hesitation. What is troubling you?"

"Perhaps I am overreacting, and it is nothing." The tip of May's tail twitched back and forth. It was definitely not "nothing."

"May, I insist you tell me now."

"My sire, Laconia, sought me out yesterday. He is concerned—well, with things that he did not wish me to repeat."

Elizabeth winced. No doubt his concerns related to Bede. "The unrest among the minor dragons."

"Yes, that, but with the unrest comes certain..."

"Attitudes and opinions?"

"Yes, those. He, of course, is not sympathetic to them, but is concerned about what he was hearing."

And he could not be seen talking to the Dragon Sage lest he be deemed untrustworthy? How tense had things become? "He wants you to leave London?"

"No, not me specifically. He suggested I be mindful of my Friend, and of you, and April, who is the smallest of our family party." May nestled her face into Elizabeth's neck.

"He believes there is a threat to us?" Pendragon's bones!

"He did not say that in so many words. But when dragons are agitated—draconic tempers being what they are—they may not be inclined to well-considered judgement."

Elizabeth ran her hand lightly along the fur on May's back. "The same is true of warm-bloods. Thank you for bringing this to my attention. I will consider what you have said."

Mrs. Sharp cleared her throat. "Would it be wise for me to prepare for—"

"A move to Darcy House, which would provide a much more comfortable environment for me as I approach my confinement." She caught Mrs. Sharp's eyes and held them until she nodded.

Nothing more needed to be said. Clearly, they understood each other.

Elizabeth left Mrs. Sharp to manage the details and descended the countless stairs to her office. May's words weighed as heavy as the stack of work that had appeared on her desk overnight. Did Chisholm ever sleep?

How much of that pile represented critical assignments and how many were nonessential tasks aimed at keeping her busy and not interfering with the Council's machinations? Dragon's bones! She had not thought of it that way, but that was exactly how it all felt.

"Good morning, Lady Sage." Chisholm peeked over the top of the heap. "I was sorting the recent correspondence."

"Adding more to the pile, I suppose?"

"Nothing unusual in that, all told. However, as we have discussed before, there is additional work which I might take on for you, if you wish. If you ask me, many of these demands reek of being ..."

"Nonessential, insignificant, frivolous?" Unfortunately, her voice had turned as bitter as too-strong tea.

Chisholm cocked her head and studied Elizabeth. "That would reduce the demands on you."

"It may be time to pursue that." Elizabeth joined Chisholm at the large, cluttered desk.

"Where do you want to begin?" Chisholm pointed out several stacks.

"Not here."

"What do you mean?" Chisholm stepped back, a crease forming between her glittering dark eyes.

"I mean to remove from here as soon as possible. The Order offices are no longer conducive to my increasingly awkward state."

"I see." Chisholm's tail swished in the way it did when she was mulling various options. "Shall I organize what needs to be taken from this office to ... Darcy House?" The way she emphasized the name—she understood the implications as clearly as Mrs. Sharp.

"Let that be your priority today."

"Yes, Lady Sage. I shall pack the relevant materials. If you like, I can ask Brutus and Axel to move crates to Darcy House as I get them collected."

"If they are available, that would be helpful. I have not decided exactly when I will remove with Little Anne, but having my office things there will hasten the process." A bit of weight lifted from her chest. How pleasant to draw a proper breath again.

"I will see to it."

"Also, keep an ear to the local gossip." Elizabeth leaned back against the edge of the desk.

"You wish me to put a stop to it?" Chisholm blinked several times as though trying to work out how to accomplish such a thing.

"No, do not interfere. I simply need to better understand what is being said. Bring me news as soon as you are made aware of it. Interrupt me as necessary, at any time."

"Indeed, Lady Sage. I will do so."

"Try to control your anxiety. It will only cause more gossip to spread." Elizabeth glanced at Chisholm's slapping tail.

"Of course. I will be more attentive to that detail. I fear you caught me by surprise..."

"Rather sudden changes in plans have marked this morning, to be sure."

"Will you still be attending the Council dragons this morning, or shall I tell them you are indisposed?"

"As much as I would rather be indisposed," Elizabeth rested her hands on her belly, "I expect they will be displeased enough to learn I am departing for ... Darcy House ... soon and will be unavailable to their beck and call."

Elizabeth did not hurry down to the courtroom—even if she had wanted to do so, it would not have been possible. At every landing she had to stop and fight dizziness and rising nausea. Whether from the exertion or the dragons who awaited her mattered little. The effect was the same. The dragons would note her increasing weakness, and that did not bode well.

She glanced up the staircase. How long would it take her to get back up when the dragons finished with her? Should she simply remove to Darcy House when she reached the ground floor and not return to the upstairs rooms at all? There were several street-level rooms at Darcy House that could be converted for her use as bedchambers. One even already had a fainting couch.

Perhaps she should leave without ever descending into the great courtroom and Council room beyond? That was tempting.

Very tempting.

But no, disappearing like that would only complicate matters. Down to the Council room she would go.

Slowly, carefully, with many stops to catch her breath and restore her composure.

Nearly there, she slowed and leaned against the cold tunnel walls. A single torch provided light from the courtroom to the Council room, only barely enough light to pick her way down the tunnel without tripping on the uneven floor. The dragons would not have needed the torch, so it was a concession, a kindness, to her warm-blooded limitations. But it hardly felt like that now.

"I come, Cownt Matlock," she called, breathless and leaning against the doorway.

"Enter." The cownt's voice rumbled and reverberated against the stone.

She lumbered in, knees unsteady and joints aching. She attempted to perform her required obeisance but hesitated—she might not be able to get back up, and it would not do to demonstrate such weakness so close to the Council dragons. So, she limited the depth of her bow and did not touch the floor.

Matlock growled deep in his throat. Dunbrook added his rumbles to Matlock's.

"I mean no disrespect, Cownt, but my condition renders me—"

"Weak?" Dunbrook hissed the word, spewing his rank breath on her face.

She swallowed bile and held her breath. No question, Dunbrook knew exactly what he was doing. Dreadful bully. "No, limited for a time. Warm-bloods carry young who grow proportionately much larger than a dragon's egg does. Imagine carrying a creature the size of a whole draft horse in your belly. It presents one with some discomfort and limitations."

"Eggssss are discomfort enough. Yours is a foolish way to produce young." Barwines Chudleigh snuffed and caught Dunbrook's and Matlock's gaze in turn. "But what you say is reassssonable."

"I assure you, had I control over it, I would find an easier alternative." Elizabeth wrapped her arms protectively around her belly.

"I will tolerate your altered display for now. That is not the reason we have summoned you." Matlock stomped his fore-foot hard enough for Elizabeth to feel through the soles of her shoes. "But ensure that the disrespect does not persist."

"Yes, Cownt."

Dunbrook snorted as though he did not believe her. "Have you addressed our concerns?"

"As I recall, you expressed alarm over several issues." She pulled her shoulders back and spine as straight as her bel-ly would allow. "I have marked the extent of Bede's dig-ging with the venom so graciously provided by Barwines Chudleigh, so there will be clear indication of additional explorations."

"You believe our demands will be honored?" Dunbrook reached his neck out toward her. A subtle threat.

"I will confirm that tomorrow, when I meet with the His-torian."

"And if it has continued, will you turn Bede over to us." Matlock did not ask a question.

"There will be no need for that."

"What do you mean?" Dunbrook's lip curled back to re-veal his fang.

"Bede has been removed from the Order offices. If further digging has taken place, it will not have been by her claws."

"Where is she?" Dunbrook's tail slapped the floor as hard as Matlock's stomp.

"I cannot tell you her precise location."

"Do not play word games with us, Sage." Matlock blew hot breath in her direction. "Where have you sent her?"

"She is at Darcy House for the time being, while final arrangements are being made to send her to a distant prop-erty with no access to the dragon tunnels."

"What assurance have you that she that will not escape?" Dunbrook asked.

"Bede is no prisoner. You ordered her away from the Archives. You did not declare her a criminal."

Dunbrook's roar echoed like cannon fire off the stone walls.

She clapped her hands to her ears. "There are three dragons and two warm-bloods assigned to keep watch over her. She is never left alone. She is to be kept occupied in the Darcy House library, cataloging the materials there."

"That isss acceptable." Chudleigh looked directly at Matlock and Dunbrook, her shimmering wings extending and tail tip flicking. "As for the other matterssss?"

Any sensible person would have beaten a hasty retreat away from the suffocating tension in the room. Elizabeth forced her feet to remain rooted in place. "Drew and Quill Driver are researching amphithere lineages, but have found little documentation of them in the records."

"What of the boxes in the old archivessss? Have you been given access to those?"

"Not yet. The Historian considers the documents he is already working on to be his priority."

"That is not acceptable," Dunbrook snarled, lips pulling back, revealing more teeth.

"Nor is your attitude, Barwin Dunbrook. I will not have it." She stomped a step closer. "I will have you remember, what you are asking of me is outside my duties as Sage. Should you be expected to survey Keep boundaries in place of the Minister of Keeps? Surely not. What you have asked of me—"

"Is necessary." Matlock thumped his tail hard enough that she jumped back. "Do not question it."

"Then do not threaten me as you would prey."

"I do not threaten prey. I simply eat it." Dunbrook muttered.

"Another threat? You have no excuse for such rudeness. I shall go." She turned. Turning one's back on angry dragons was not widely considered wisdom.

"No," Matlock said. "The issue remains. We need to know what is in those crates."

Elizabeth looked over her shoulder.

"Pray, tell the Historian there is reason for me to believe there are portraitssss somewhere in those crates that can confirm my claims to my Keep. Tell him I need those answers immediately." Chudleigh's expression warned Elizabeth not to argue.

Oh, but it was so tempting! "There are many crates, Barwines. How might the most likely candidates be identified?"

Chudleigh glared in grudging approval. "Find a tatzelwurm to ssssmell for paint."

"Is it not likely to be exceedingly faint by now? What variety of paint should they be trying to identify?"

"Blue. Order-blue paint."

12
Chapter

AFTER LEAVING THE COUNCIL, Elizabeth regarded the flights of steps up to the ground floor of the Order offices. The weight on her shoulders expanded like a dragon vying for dominance, filling the stairwell, forcing her down, until her knees gave way, and she sat upon the lowest step. The stone's cold radiated through her dress, to her bones, to her soul itself.

What were the Council dragons about? What did they really want from within the Archives? Why did they not want to tell her the truth?

And how did she feel about that?

Dragons, like men, usually had their own agendas. Some were well informed, well intended, well thought out. Some were not. Some were to be trusted. Some were not.

What was the case here?

Were the Council's Keepers aware of what their Dragon Mates were meeting about, or were they kept at an even greater distance than Elizabeth? Clearly, the warm-blooded, non-Council officers had not been told anything. Perhaps their dragons were similarly uninformed. Considering the way major dragons managed their Keeps—sharing as little information as possible with anyone of lesser status than themselves—it was not difficult to imagine the Council dragons managed Council affairs the same way.

It was not as though she could ask anyone about that.

Just because the Council wanted things a certain way did not mean she had to comply. Yes, good sense and self-preservation suggested she should, but that could not stop her from wondering whether it was the right choice to do as they said without question. They had their own priorities, but who would benefit from them?

And how was she to understand any of it? How had things become so complicated?

"Are you well, Lady Sage?" Drew slipped into the stairwell from the courtroom. Clumps of dust dotted his long, green nose.

"Merely tired, thank you." She braced her hands on the step and straightened her shoulders.

"Is it long before you lay ... that is, produce your young?" He cocked his head and blinked as though that were the most polite and natural of questions.

"Cownt Matlock declared it would be several months yet, but," she ran her hand over her belly, "it may be sooner than that."

Drew's tail swished. "Will you be nesting soon?"

"Yes, I plan to."

"You will choose somewhere safe for you and your young to remain undisturbed?"

"That is the intent of a woman's lying-in. Forgive me, but I am surprised by your concern. This is not my first birth."

He edged back half a bit. "Pray, do not be offended, Lady Sage. We are merely concerned for you."

We? Who was "we?" "I am not offended, to be sure. Only puzzled at your level of alarm."

"Surely you have felt the tension in the air. The Council dragons are keeping secrets again, and it is never a positive thing when they do."

"It happens often?" Tread lightly! Tread lightly! Do not scare him off.

"Enough. Usually when—" he mouthed the words 'the Brenin,' "—is about to make an ill-advised decision. It is not unusual for those to be grievous for—" mouthing again 'minor dragons.'

"I did not realize. So, you have been through this before?"

"Several times, but none as troubling as now." He glanced over his shoulder, ears twitching.

"And how did those situations resolve?"

"Better than might have been hoped for. If one did not know better, one might complain, but if one could properly hypothesize what might have been, one would not."

"So you trust—" she mouthed 'the Council?'

"It could be much worse." He looked down as he worried his front paws. "What brings you underground when it is so uncomfortable for you?"

"Is my father in the Archives today?"

"No, he is not. He was not strong enough today. Perhaps tomorrow."

"Might I—"

"The Scribe is not in the Archives, either."

"Meaning no one is welcome in that space without one of them present?"

"Other than Bylock and myself, and of course, Bede, but no one has seen her today." Drew's eyes asked the question.

"I am sure she is quite well." Elizabeth grabbed the handrail and pulled herself to her feet. "Pray, send me word when my father is next in the Archives. Perhaps even go so far as to recommend he get there as soon as he is able?"

"Is there something you need from there? I could get it for you. It is well within my authority to do that." He looked so hopeful. It was probably difficult to deny the Dragon Sage.

"I will keep that in mind but, for now, no. What I need must be accomplished in person."

"Do you require help upstairs?"

"Thank you for the offer, but I require a bit of time alone."

Drew's head crest drooped, but he kept his disappointment to himself as he scurried up the stairs ahead of her.

What a strange conversation on multiple levels. That she was denied access to the Archives was strange and worrisome, full stop. But in some ways, not altogether surprising. However, the discussion she did not have with Drew—that was eye-opening.

The confirmation that the Council was prone to secrecy was hardly a surprise. But Drew's observations about Londinium—those were unexpected to say the least. How widespread were those observations—how many dragons, major or minor, had concerns about their Brenin's governance? And why had they not shared them with her?

That question stuck like a pebble in her shoe, sharp and painful.

Drew seemed to trust the Council, though, that their decisions would be better than the Brenin's, even if imperfect themselves. His confidence should have quelled some of the roiling in her belly.

Should have.

Unfortunately, the bigger issue of what precisely their actions were and what they were better than lingered like a basilisk stalking its prey.

The next morning, Elizabeth sat in her parlor rocking chair with Little Anne and May, whilst Mrs. Sharp, Mercy, and Truth finished packing the nursery. Paragons of efficiency, all of them. Brutus was off finalizing arrangements with the Blue Order office staff dragons to transport her things to Darcy House via the dragon tunnels. The less attention drawn to the event, the better. With the Blue Order office atmosphere growing ever more stifling, Elizabeth needed space to reflect and breathe and be away from the air of threat and secrecy spreading in every corner.

Little Anne stood, in unsteady toddler fashion, in the middle of the worn carpet that covered most of the parlor floor, giggling as May chased her tail. May had often tail-chased as a young wyrmling. It was hard to know whether she did so now for Little Anne's sake or for her own amusement. Either way, it was fun to watch as she turned somersaults across the floor in the quest to snare her prey.

Little Anne clapped and toddled to Elizabeth, grinning and cooing. She stumbled. Somehow, May managed to catch Anne before she fell, helping her regain her balance and be on her way again. Anne hugged May, perhaps a mite harder than she should, but May purred and flicked her tail contentedly. Tatzelwurms were much sturdier than mere cats.

This was what the Order was supposed to be like, with warm- and cold-blooded members working together to the betterment of all. Enjoying one another's company, assisting one another, with no need to question motives or agendas.

Could it ever be that way? Perhaps it was the height of naïveté to believe so.

Little Anne raised her arms and looked at Elizabeth, who lifted Anne into her lap. There was nothing like cuddling a warm, wriggling toddler, smelling of roses, lavender, and dragon musk. Soon Anne would be too big for such things, so best enjoy it as much as she could now, before Anne's childhood innocence faded away to be replaced with more mature pursuits.

Maybe Elizabeth's innocence about the Order was ending now, too. Maybe Elizabeth was finally growing up and coming into those unpleasant realizations that came with adulthood.

She had considered herself mature and clear-sighted, but perhaps not as much as she had thought.

Would she now become as cynical and hardened as Papa? Heaven forefend!

Anne looked up at her, a troubled little look furrowing her brow.

"No, my dear, nothing is wrong. You are everything delightful and perfect." Elizabeth hugged Little Anne tight. "That is all I need to think about right now. And we are soon to go back to Darcy House to enjoy more of this. Would you like to visit Amber and Slate? They would like to see you again."

"Dwagns?" Little Anne's first word had been 'dragons'. Somehow that was fitting.

"Yes, they are dragon friends."

"Fwend? May?" She pointed at the tatzelwurm, whose ears pricked and tail tip twitched in answer.

"Friends, but not like May. May is your special Friend, like April is mine."

"Apl? See Apl?" She looked around the room. "No see!"

"She is not here, but I hope she will be here soon. She went to see Papa."

"Papa? Want Papa!" Anne pushed off Elizabeth's lap to search the room. She crawled under the table and peered beneath the settee.

"He is not here. But perhaps we will see him soon."

May stopped tumbling, planted her feet, and trotted up to Elizabeth. "Is Keeper coming to London?" Since Pemberley called Darcy Keeper, little May had adopted the practice. Though some might argue it was improper, it was May's best way to express her respect and trust for him, so they did not press her to change. "I thought he was still at Pemberley."

"I have not received word that he is coming to London."

"Then why might you see him soon? What I said ... are you planning—"

Elizabeth huffed a growly sound. Her narrowed eyes caught May's gaze. "I have no plans, nor intentions. Do not suggest that I do. Do you understand?" She pulled herself up straight and flared her elbows.

"Yes, Lady Sage, I understand." May stretched out her paws and touched her chin to the floor. Not technically the correct response, but it conveyed her intentions well enough.

Had another tatzelwurm offered such a response, Elizabeth would have been careful to clarify exactly what could and could not be said. But May was as sensible and clever as Laconia and could be trusted far more than the average tatzelwurm, young or old.

The servants' door inched open. Drew entered, with Brutus close behind.

Drew scurried up to her and dropped his chin to the floor. "Lady Sage, you asked me to tell you when the Historian was in the Archives. He just arrived there, but I do not know how long he will remain, so if you wish to visit the Archives, perhaps it would be best—"

"Understood." Elizabeth pushed up off the arms of the rocking chair and held the small of her back, hissing. Oh, this was growing tiresome!

Brutus bounded to her side. "Should you be going down yourself, Lady Sage?"

"I have no choice. I must."

"Then I will accompany you." Brutus had that look. There would be no changing his mind.

"Of course. Give me a moment to alert Mrs. Sharp of our plans. May, I need for you to accompany us as well."

"Me?" May's eyes widened as she rose high on her tail.

"Yes, I need your help on a matter for with which you are uniquely qualified to assist me."

Brutus nosed May lightly. Was that encouragement in his eyes? Such a friendship between the two. Did either of them realize that was exactly the sort of reminder she needed right now?

Chapter 13

THE TRIP DOWNSTAIRS SEEMED remarkably more difficult than it had the day before. It had not been this way when she was pregnant with Anne. She had been at Pemberley then, with far fewer stairs to manage, so maybe that was the reason it seemed worse. But she felt so much bigger now. Perhaps Matlock—how much could he really understand about human birth?—was off in his estimate of Baby Darcy's arrival.

Brutus' help proved more valuable than she would prefer to admit, offering his strong shoulder and insisting on stopping and resting, when she would ordinarily have pressed on. All three dragons with her saw what he was about, and joined his efforts, with all the subtlety dragons were capable of. Their support made the journey easier, though by no means easy. She gulped air and lumbered like an ancient wyvern, tempted to moan about the aches and pains by the time they reached the end of the long, irregular tunnel to the oldest rooms of the Archives.

Elizabeth stepped over the threshold into the main room, but it had changed in her absence. She leaned heavily against the opening and stared, trying to identify the alterations. An extra torch lit the chamber, illuminating the hole that Bede had dug in the back wall. Old grey bricks, which had been removed from the wall, were piled nearby, hinting that an effort to restore them might be made. Was Papa trying to hide Bede's discovery?

A disheveled Lady Astrid stood near a worktable piled with documents. What was wrong with her? Aside from frequent dust on her gown, which was an occupational hazard, she had all the poise and composure of a fashion plate, ready to step off the page and get to business. But today her body was tense and her movements stiff and over-controlled, as though she were trying to avoid a predator.

Papa sat on a short wooden crate, clumsily rummaging through an open crate, muttering to himself, hair disordered and dusty coat rumpled. His movements, always slow and careful when he handled artifacts, seemed haphazard and even a touch random.

Brutus dragged a stool toward her, his expression strongly suggesting that she should sit down. No matter how much she wanted to argue, he was right; better to accept it gracefully than elevate the tension in the confined room.

Papa looked up at her with eyes that somehow did not seem his own. Usually they were clear, bright, quick, and clever. Was it a trick of the light that their blue was paler and ... vacant? "What are you doing here? Have you not disrupted my work enough?"

"I only now walked in. How can I have disrupted anything?"

Lady Astrid stepped close and laid her hand on Elizabeth's shoulder as Brutus edged closer.

"The Lady Sage has need of your assistance, Historian." Drew approached Papa.

"Help, she wants? Now, after what she has done?"

"What do you believe she has done?" Lady Astrid asked in a tone far more politic than she typically used with Papa.

"I cannot fathom how you would so blindly allow the Council—"

So sharp and angry and she had not even said good morning yet! "What are you talking about, Papa?" May pressed against her leg. Was that in protection of Elizabeth, or seeking protection from Papa—or maybe a little of both?

"Bede! Or had you not noticed she is not here right now?" He stood on wobbly legs, bracing himself against Drew's shoulder.

"The only thing I have noticed is your rude greeting." She winced as the words left her mouth.

"You will not speak to me in such a manner, Lizzy." He tried to move closer, but Drew blocked his way.

"If you want courtesy, then you should employ it yourself, Historian Bennet." No, not how a daughter was to address her father, at least not by warm-blooded standards. But there were dragons present, and she was not about to concede dominance in front of them, especially when acting in her role as Dragon Sage.

Blasted nuisance when warm- and cold-blood conventions contradicted each other.

"I suppose you want me to refer to you as Lady Elizabeth then, or perhaps Lady Sage as the dragons do?" Papa snorted and sneered.

"Both of you, that is enough." Lady Astrid slipped between them, extending her arms wide. "You are both on the same side here." She threw a pleading glance at Elizabeth.

"Why should I believe that after what she has done?"

"What transgression do you charge me with?" And what was wrong with him? As disagreeable as he could be, this was still out of character.

"You sent Bede away, exactly when I most need her help. You let them send her away with no consideration for my work."

"That is not fair, Historian." Drew shoved the short crate against the back of Papa's legs and tugged at his sleeve to encourage him to sit.

"Is that what you believe? Then you are short-sighted indeed," Elizabeth said.

"What is that supposed to mean?"

"I was the one who sent her to you to help you with your efforts in the first place. I tell you often how valuable I regard your efforts to be. Have I not always supported you, even helping craft the arrangements that allowed you to stay in London, near your beloved Library?"

He sniffed and rolled his eyes. "You did not appreciate Bede as you should. No doubt you did not argue her case sufficiently to the Council. Admit it now."

Enough already! "I admit to saving her life; that is what I admit to."

"What do you mean?" Papa sat heavily on the crate, nearly toppling backward.

"If you will stop your ranting and listen for a moment, I will remind you of the conversation we recently had."

Drew winced and shook his head hard. Lady Astrid touched Elizabeth's elbow, mirroring Drew's expression.

"Lizzy—"

"Pray, remind us all of that, Lady Elizabeth," Lady Astrid said.

Brutus stationed himself in front of her stool, not blocking her view of Papa, but ready to spring into action. In one way, it was comforting, but deeply unsettling at the same time.

Elizabeth rubbed her forehead. "As I told you, the situation is complicated. In short, Bede crossed the Council too many times. Between that and her digging out the Archives, they have deemed her intolerable. They declared that if they saw her again, it would be the last time." She let the threat hang in the air.

She had not used quite those words before, but perhaps being draconically direct would jog Papa's memory.

"Balderdash. They could have said no such thing."

"I am afraid they did." Elizabeth glanced at May.

May step-slithered ahead of Brutus and leaned hard against his strong front legs. "With respect, sir, they said exactly that. They were threatening to eat her if she crossed paths with them again."

"That is illegal." Papa's eyes narrowed as he glared at May. "You must have misheard. Everyone knows a tatzelwurm—"

"This tatzelwurm is entirely reliable." Brutus muttered loud enough to be heard.

Elizabeth pressed her knee against Brutus' shoulder. His defense of his friend was admirable, and probably something Papa needed to hear, but not wholly proper. "The Council is free to do what it will in some arenas, and one of those is regarding annoying minor dragons whom few hold in high regard and whom even fewer respect."

Papa sagged like a lumpy sack of potatoes, the ire draining from his face. The proud Order officer was now replaced with a tired, and perhaps even frightened, old man. "Where is she? Is she safe?"

"She is at Darcy House, under constant watch by the staff dragons. I have arranged for Sir Frederick to take her with him to Kellynch-by-the-Sea when he departs. She will be of help in sorting out the Blue Order office there. There is a rumor that extensive information on sea dragons exists in their archives." Elizabeth held her breath, watching him.

He scratched his head and raked back his hair. "But Lyme? That is so distant. She cannot assist me."

"Distance is exactly the point. There are no dragon tunnels to Kellynch-by-the-Sea. It will be difficult for her to return to London."

"Which is what she needs. The poor dear lacks the sense to recognize when her own hide is in danger." Lady Astrid nodded too vigorously, her tone too bright.

"I need her for the work I am doing." Confidence slipped from his shoulders and scattered on the rough floor.

"But you know the Council dragons, Papa. Her life is in danger if she stays. She has not the control to manage discreetly under the circumstances. Surely you have another scribe—"

"Whom I can trust? Who has the knowledge and memory that she does? Whose dedication rivals hers? No, I do not. There is no one else in the Order who can do what she can. What is so difficult about understanding her value?"

"I sent her to Darcy House, out of the immediate reach of the Council, because I value her. Why do you not accept that?" Elizabeth tried to rise and go to him, but Brutus pressed her back.

"I do not understand your work here." May asked, eyes round and fur fluffed. She had learned sometimes cute-and-adorable was a viable strategy for dealing with difficult souls. "What do you need Bede's help with?"

"She is the most effective dragon script translator I have ever met. The items she uncovered will take years to translate without her help." Papa glanced around the room, eyes stopping on pile after pile of documents.

May mewed sweetly. "Could you send some of the writings with her?"

"Allow scrolls and books out of the Archives?" Papa gasped as though an apoplectic fit were not far off.

Lady Astrid hurried beside him. "Wait, wait, before you go off on another tear, let us examine the idea carefully."

"There is nothing to consider. The hazards to the materials—"

"Yes, it is real, Papa." Elizabeth stood, a subtle reminder of dominance. "But have you thought of the danger they may be in if they remain here?"

"You must be joking. You cannot be serious."

"Forgive me for intruding, but she has a point," Drew said.

"What are you talking about?" Papa all but snarled into Drew's face, but Drew only blinked.

What a patient dragon. "Anyone who can make it to the Archives will be able to find the new room that Bede discovered, no matter how well we try to disguise it." Drew glanced over his shoulder at the pile of bricks.

"But who would—"

"If the Council is feeling threatened, then they might have reason to send loyal operatives ..." Lady Astrid swallowed hard.

Papa sputtered and huffed, but clearly, he had not considered the possibility.

"If you can pack up those documents and dispatch them to the Lyme Office, which is Blue Order territory, they would not leave the custody of the Order, but would be available for her to translate," Elizabeth said.

"But would they understand how to manage such articles safely?"

"Bede does." Elizabeth stepped around Brutus toward Papa. "And we can send instructions that she is the only one to handle the materials. I am certain Lady Wentworth and her Friend, Balen, will ensure their safety. They are trustworthy."

Papa rocked on the stool, chewing his lower lip. "Lady Wentworth has a healthy respect for archival documents and for our history."

"I trust her," Lady Astrid said. "It is a good option, considering the circumstances."

Papa fidgeted and huffed. "Yes, yes, I suppose there is little alternative. Drew, come with me. There are books and scrolls to identify and prepare."

"Wait." Lady Astrid lifted a hand. "We have not inquired what has brought you here, Lady Elizabeth. Surely, this is not an ordinary morning call."

"No, I am afraid not. The Council is interested in the crates in the Archives. Specifically, Barwines Chudleigh is interested in portraits that might help establish her claim to her territory."

"There have been challenges?" Papa cocked his head, brows knitting.

"She has expressed her concern." Hopefully, he would ask no more.

"Very well, go snoop about to your heart's content. Make the Barwines happy as you will. I will resume my business. Brutus, would you be available to help deal with transport to Darcy House?"

Brutus glanced at Elizabeth, who nodded. "I am at your disposal, Historian."

Papa grunted and trundled off into Bede's most recent tunnel. Why, though? Had he not said they had removed everything of interest from there already?

"Where do you want to begin?" Lady Astrid asked.

"With him." Elizabeth dropped her voice to a whisper and chin-pointed toward Papa. "What was that all about? I discussed the matter with him already. It is not like him—"

"Unfortunately, it is."

No! She could not have just said that. "What do you mean? Have these memory lapses been a regular occurrence?"

"They become more regular when he is agitated, less so when things are less tense. You must understand how trying the atmosphere has been. For all that he declares her necessary, Bede is still difficult. Especially with one after another of the staff coming to him to complain. And now with the Council and their crankiness,—well, everyone is on edge and not at their best."

"What I saw was more than Papa not being at his best, though."

"That was a more extreme outburst, to be sure. It is not usually so bad as that." Lady Astrid shrugged as though to apologize.

"Do you fear he is losing his faculties?"

"Not yet."

"Not yet? How long?"

"There is no way to predict." Lady Astrid stared at her hands. "I confess, I spoke to Sir Edward about it before he left. Your father has not been eating well since he came to London. As I understand, he often skips meals and eats only a few things. He says the cook at Middleset House is—well, I shall not repeat his exact words, but he finds her services wanting. Sir Edward thinks the problem may relate to poor digestion. It might not be what you fear."

"That is some hope. I will write to Sir Edward and inquire further." Elizabeth pressed her temples. One more thing to deal with.

"What was it you came for this morning? It would be best to get to it before he returns."

"Yes, that. May, will you please check the crates for Order-blue paint?" Elizabeth gestured at May, who spring-hopped to the nearest crate, and sniffed it.

"Blue paint? She can detect that?"

"Not any blue, Order-blue. Tatzelwurms have an acute sense of smell, and that particular paint has a component with a distinct odor."

"Oh, I had forgotten." Lady Astrid stepped back and gestured for May to continue.

May slithered around crates and trunks and shelves as she sniffed her way through the room. She paused in the far corner.

"There is a great deal of Order-blue here." She tapped her front feet on the box she stood upon.

"We have not begun cataloging that area." Lady Astrid blew out a strained breath. "I am not sure—"

"Pray, no discussion. The Council has ordered it. They will not be gainsaid."

"At least allow me to open the crates properly to minimize any damage." Lady Astrid retrieved a pry bar from a shelf in the corner.

Elizabeth picked her way to the far corner. May stood atop the largest crate, dusty and worn, surrounded by several smaller ones. Dragon script markings Elizabeth could not decipher danced around the top edge of each. "All three contain Order-blue."

"Hop down, and I will start with the largest one." Lady Astrid pointed with her pry bar. She pried loose the narrow side of the largest crate. "Mind the nails there." She set the side panel aside. "Paintings, as you expected, May. Let us see what we have here." She slid out a painting, still mounted in a gilded frame. "Definitely an amphithere. I do not recognize the background, but perhaps the Barwines will. There is a bit of an inscription on the frame. Appears to be a name and a location, and a date? I should be able to sort that out quickly enough. I wonder what else we have here."

A portrait of another amphithere and presumably its Keeper. A landscape of an estate or Keep. It was difficult to tell which in the uneven torchlight. A portrait of father and son with what may have been an amphithere in flight in the background. Interesting.

"Barwines Chudleigh should be satisfied with those." No, probably not, but they provided evidence that her request was well founded.

"Perhaps we ought to wait to identify what these inscriptions say before going that far." Lady Astrid chuckled. "But either way, these are interesting indeed. Dragon portraits like that one are rare. Should we check the other crates?"

"Yes, yes," May step-slithered around an unimpressive short box, rubbing her furry black cheek against it. "This one."

Lady Astrid worked the lid off. "None of these are framed. They will need to be unrolled carefully."

"Wait, wait." May jumped to the edge of the crate and sniffed each of the rolled canvases. "Start with these three. They smell the strongest."

"As she says." Elizabeth bit her knuckle.

"We ought to go back to the table to unroll these. The light is better there." Lady Astrid gathered up the canvases and trundled back.

Elizabeth cleared space for the paintings.

May's fur and body pouffed and her forked tongue flicked the air. What had her so alarmed?

"These three are tied together with a blue ribbon." Lady Astrid placed the canvases on the table. "I would rather untie it than cut it. If you will be patient for a moment, let me see what I can do."

Elizabeth pulled her stool close and sat on her hands lest she interfere. May hopped onto the table but kept her distance from Lady Astrid's work, though the twitch of her ears revealed her impatience.

"There now, I have it." The ribbon fell away and the three rolls rolled along the rough-hewn table. "Where do we start?" She picked up the leftmost canvas and unrolled it. "It looks like it was part of a triptych." She pointed at the arched shape, painted in gold and Order-blue, along the top of the canvas. "Oh heavens! May, pray bring the Historian. Quickly!"

May mewed and leapt off the table and disappeared into the shadows.

"I cannot believe it. Do you know what this is?" Lady Astrid held down the edges of the canvas. "The man and the red dragon? This is Uther Pendragon and Dewi, and on the table between them, those are the Accords!"

"How can you tell?"

"The shield here, near Uther, that is his coat of arms. And this glyph in dragon script, it is the symbol for Dewi. There is no doubt. I cannot believe this! What a treasure this is!"

"A treasure, you say?" Papa called from the shadows. "Out of my way! Let me examine it."

Brutus rushed to his side to keep him from tripping.

"The Pendragon Accords—this must be the original work I have read about, of the signing of the Treaty! It has been missing for so long, right under our feet! Surely the Council—"

"No, Papa, wait, please." Elizabeth pressed a hand to her mouth, a chill creeping along the back of her neck. "Do you not see?"

"What are you blithering about?"

"Dewi! Look at him."

"What is wrong? He is clearly the red dragon in the picture." Papa stabbed his finger toward the image, not touching it.

"But his size, his size! He is not depicted as a major dragon at all. Look at him next to Uther. He is barely larger than your Friend Bylock, is he not, Lady Astrid?" Elizabeth pressed both hands to her heart.

Papa waved off her idea. "Paintings of this age have issues with scale. Individuals of equal import would be depicted in the same size. Surely that is what we are seeing here."

"Unroll the others, please." Elizabeth shook her head.

Papa and Lady Astrid each took a canvas and opened it.

"Look at the major dragons!" Elizabeth pointed at the one Papa held open. Very large major dragons, all in correct proportion, filled the image. "And the minor ones." The one Lady Astrid held was covered with every variety of minor dragon. "It is not a matter of proportion. The other dragons are depicted properly. And the frontmost dragon on each of those panels holds a quill as if to sign the Accords as representative for their types. It makes little sense that they would be captured accurately, but the most important figures, Uther and Dewi, are not."

Papa clutched the table, gasping. Brutus shoved a stool under him as his knees collapsed. "No, this cannot be. It is not possible."

"All our records report Dewi was a major dragon, a red fire-drake." Lady Astrid's voice was thin, barely audible. "He could not have been so diminutive."

"It is possible." Elizabeth clenched and unclenched her hands. "Consider what we know about Dewi, that his dominance was acknowledged because of his understanding and wisdom, with little or no reference to his size. Just as with me. I am hardly a major dragon, so perhaps neither was he. In this painting it looks like he is not even the size of Bolsover, the smallest of England's firedrakes."

"But he is larger than the minor dragons pictured. So, he must be a major dragon." Papa tried to sound authoritative but failed.

"Even if that is the case, Papa, notice the quill in the minor dragon's hand. A representative of the minor dragons signed the Accords."

"But there is no record of that."

"But that would mean..." Lady Astrid said.

"That would mean that, just possibly, everything we believe about the relations between major and minor dragons is wrong," Elizabeth whispered. "No wonder the Council has been so agitated."

14
Chapter

ELIZABETH PEEKED INTO EACH of the boxes and trunks piled in the nursery, taking note of what each one held. Despite Mrs. Sharp's thorough efficiency, there was still something soothing about going over everything with her own eyes and hands. Perhaps it was too many experiences with her mother and Lydia when what was planned and what actually happened did not match and being the person everyone turned to when it all went pear-shaped. To be fair, Lydia had gotten much better about such things, though Kitty had readily taken her place.

How different it was, traveling with her mother and sisters, rare as those events might have been. Oh, the piles of trunks and boxes and bags. The last-minute flurry of demands that lost items be found, borrowed ones returned, and damaged ones mended. The shoe roses! The hair ribbons! A favorite spencer that both Kitty and Lydia wanted to wear. And the hats! So many hats!

By comparison, the stack in the nursery seemed meager and insufficient for her station as Lady Elizabeth Darcy. But without Darcy's company and steadily increasing, she had not intended to take part in the social season, so she had brought little in the way of full dress. She rarely walked out; the security risks made Brutus nearly frantic. So only one walking dress had come with her from Pemberley. And since the winters in London were milder than in Derbyshire, her warmest things had stayed behind as well. Everything she needed fit into just a few sturdy trunks.

No, not everything she needed, not even remotely.

She dragged the back of her hand across her eyes. Silly, sentimental woman. Those things left at Pemberley were not lost—those things and all the people she had left behind would be there for her when she returned.

Merciful heavens, that needed to be soon.

And it would be. This afternoon, a maid from Darcy House would organize the transfer of her belongings out of the Order offices.

Then she would have to tell the Council dragons of the change. That would not be a pleasant conversation. All the more reason to avoid it for a little longer. Still, she could not put it off forever.

If only she understood what was bothering the Council, it would be easier to work out how best to approach them with the news. But they were so close-fanged right now. Not that it was uncharacteristic for dragons to be so—that was the way of important men, too—but they usually trusted her enough to give some indications.

She rubbed her upper arms as she wandered from the nursery to the parlor and eased into her comfortable rocking chair. The wooden joints creaked as she sat down and leaned back. The soft sound straddled the line between a complaint and a welcome, familiar and warm. Too bad Anne was on a walk with Mrs. Sharp in the courtyard behind the office, a place so well-guarded by multiple dragons that even Brutus felt it safe enough to let them walk on their own. Though Little Anne needed time in the sunshine, Elizabeth's arms ached to hold her, cuddle her, and be reminded that all was not cold and scaly in the world.

The baby she carried wriggled and kicked, perhaps sensing his mother's desires.

"No, I have not forgotten about you, little one." She stroked her belly and Baby Darcy settled.

May step-slithered out from the shadows, Brutus following. Odd that May was not out with her Friend. How long had they been there watching her? And what were they watching for? She could ask, of course, but most likely she would receive a polite, politic answer, designed not to further worry her with unnecessary musings from the minor dragons of her entourage.

"Your offspring is uneasy." May rose on her tail, asking permission to hop into Elizabeth's lap.

She patted her thigh and May sprang up. "That happens from time to time." She ran her fingers along the lush black fur on May's shoulders.

"This is different. He is uneasy. He can sense the changes; that things are difficult now." May pressed against her belly and purred.

Was that to say the dragon knew something and was asking permission to speak? "What do you mean by changes?"

"She is right." Brutus sat on his haunches beside Elizabeth and nosed May, who rubbed her cheek against his snout. Such an unlikely pair, those two, and yet, bordering on inseparable.

"The Archives ..." May whispered.

Elizabeth leaned close to May's ear. "No, say nothing, not even here."

"She is right." Brutus nosed May again, and she huffed. "Action may be required."

"I am not certain if it is time for that, yet. I am certain it will be clear when the time is right, though." Elizabeth soothed May's ruffled fur.

"I do not like it. For many reasons." Brutus's tail swept broad strokes along the carpet, swishing and pricking as dry scales caught against the fibers.

"I do not fault you for that." She disliked it, too, but it would not be helpful to expound upon that at the moment. "For now, though, I must await Sir Frederick."

"He has been ordered away." May circled in Elizabeth's lap.

"How would you know that?"

"The Council met with him not long ago—"

"May! You are spying on the Council?" Foolish wyrmling! Those were exactly the rash actions that were likely to—

"No, she was not." Brutus slapped his tail on the floor.

"Laconia told me." May mewed as she rose on her serpentine tail and looked Elizabeth in the eye. "Sir Frederick told him. And Laconia is none too happy about it."

"What do you mean? What troubles him?" Tiny prickles gathered along the back of Elizabeth's neck.

"Everything." Brutus grumbled.

"You were privy to their conversation?"

"He hardly lets me out of his sight." May swatted at Brutus' nose.

All things considered, that was probably for the best.

"With good reason." Brutus laid his front paw on the arm of the rocker. "Laconia does not like the Council's plan for dealing with Cornwall."

"Sir Frederick approaches. Perhaps you should discuss it with him." May hopped off Elizabeth's lap and spring-hopped to the door.

Brutus followed and opened it before Sir Frederick knocked.

How kind of them not to trouble her with answering for herself, ensuring she did as they asked. She pinched her temples and shook her head.

Sir Frederick registered no surprise at the suddenly-open door. He bowed and entered, Laconia close behind. "Thank you for seeing me on such short notice, Lady Elizabeth."

She braced on the chair's arms, then thought better of it. "Forgive me if I do not rise."

"Of course." He moved to the overstuffed chair nearest hers. "Did I tell you that Lady Wentworth shares your happy state?"

"No, I did not realize. Congratulations to both of you." She would have to write to Anne and ask her about their plans to introduce their infant to dragons. If she shared the Darcys' views, they might start an alternative approach to raising the next generation of the Blue Order. "I hope your travels do not keep you away from her long."

"There is no way of telling, I am afraid. But for now, I am grateful for the excuse to stop at Kellynch-by-the-Sea as I conduct my next mission for the Order."

"Please send her my regards." Elizabeth glanced from the tatzelwurms to Brutus, her finger pressed to her lips.

They nodded and dispersed. Elizabeth and Sir Frederick continued their idle conversation until all three peeked in and indicated it was not safe to speak.

Not safe to speak.

Blast and botheration.

Sir Frederick scowled, his lips wrinkling into a thoughtful frown. Elizabeth held up one finger as she rose and waddled—bless it all, she was waddling now—to the nursery, bringing back a child's slate from one of the trunks.

We can use this, she wrote and handed the slate and pencil to Sir Frederick. He nodded, a small lift to his lips in his otherwise somber expression.

It was nice that he appreciated making use of what was on hand, even if it was unconventional.

"I hope you have pleasant travels to her. If you like, I have a receipt for a favorite stomach-soothing tea that she might find useful."

"What a thoughtful gesture," he said as he wrote: Allister Salt has arranged for our safe travel.

May patrolled the windowsills, Laconia stretched out across the door to the hall, and Brutus stationed himself at the servants' door.

"I regard your wife quite highly. I have heard she has a Friend now." Will there be sufficient room to transport several trunks of sensitive items as well?

"Her name is Balen. She is a most extraordinary cockatrix, unlike any I have ever met. She has a most extraordinary story." Salt thinks it unwise to transport items in ordinary luggage. He acquired trunks with false bottoms to be delivered to Darcy House this afternoon.

"I have heard that Balen looks unlike most greater cockatrix. I imagine her story is quite unusual as well. Pray tell me more. There is nothing more fascinating than a dragon's stories."

Sir Frederick launched into a spirited telling of Balen's history—which was absolutely fascinating, and unlike any Elizabeth had ever heard.

Definitely a dragon she needed to spend more time with. "How is she settling into her new life at Kellynch-by-the-Sea?" I will have the items brought to Darcy House as soon as we conclude our meeting.

"Very well, all things considered. As for Balen's history..." Sir Frederick wiped away her remark and wrote: Your guest is still intending to travel to Lyme?

Yes. She is prepared to travel at a moment's notice. Axel will accompany her. She is difficult and distractible and needs someone to keep a close watch on her.

Sir Frederick's brow creased as he wrote more slowly. Will she need a companion in Lyme?

Possibly. How did one briefly explain a dragon like Bede? But if put to work that she finds interesting and useful, she should be fine.

What sort of tasks would you suggest? Will Wynn be able to provide such employment?

Elizabeth shook her head. Mr. Wynn might be effective in his position, but creativity and nonstandard approaches were not in his list of strengths. The items you are transporting should suffice for her.

The nature of these items?

Of greater value than I can express. They are best kept secure. I recommend a basement at Kellynch.

Not in the Order offices?

No, not safe enough. No one else must know of them, beyond you and Lady W and your Friends.

What of Kellynch? Despite his injuries, he will have to accept our guest in his territory. What may I tell him? Given his history, I do not relish deception of any kind.

I trust you to determine what is most appropriate. The more he is aware of, the greater the risk of the Council's ire toward him.

I will consult with Anne. Her insight is excellent. "And that is how Balen came to us."

"What an extraordinary adventure. I should like to meet Balen someday."

"After my mission is complete, you are, of course, welcome at Kellynch-by-the-Sea any time. I am certain Kellynch would be honored by your notice, and Anne prizes your friendship."

"Give her my regards when you see her. Is Kellynch going to be a part of your latest mission?"

Sir Frederick wiped away the last scribble on the slate and set it on the floor near his chair. "It seems unwise. He is not in Cornwall's good graces. Council business requires that I pay a call upon Dug Cornwall himself."

Elizabeth swallowed hard. That was not an errand she would relish. "Regarding the matter of Chesil, I expect?"

"I suppose it is rather obvious when one is aware of what actually happened in Lyme." He raked his fingers through his hair. "It will not surprise you that the situation is rather delicate. Cownt Matlock has himself penned a letter to Dug Cornwall, in Matlock's capacity of Grand Dug."

"Oh, that is serious! He does not like to flaunt that title unnecessarily." And who could blame him? A flagrant show of dominance was sure to provoke a corresponding display.

"Most serious. Of course, I have not been made privy to the letter's contents. I am only the messenger, but it does not take a great deal of imagination to guess Dug Cornwall will not be pleased." Sir Frederick's neutral tone, neutral expression, and neutral posture revealed the depth of his concerns.

"No, he will not." Elizabeth tried to match his calm, but sheer determination was no match for his years of calm in the face of death-defying experience. "You will have witnesses with you, no?"

"I doubt they will have much impact on the Dug, but yes, the Council shares your concern. I am to be met there at Land's End by a security team of large minor drakes to serve as bondsmen, if you will, to remind Cornwall that I am a protected agent of the Order. At the least, they will provide witnesses to the Council of his behavior, should it come to that, which I very much hope it does not. But if nothing else, the witnesses will enable them to ensure justice is done."

Cold and hollow, the words hung in the air, then fell, splintering on the floor. To be offered as that sort of sacrifice... "I am sorry such an errand is necessary." And more sorry for his wife and baby-to-be who might never meet its father.

He shrugged, resigned, or at least wearing the appearance of it. "Such is the lot of a military man, or a former military man, in my case." He reached for the slate. "I must finish my preparations to be off, if you will excuse me. Thank you for your condescension and good wishes." I shall send Balen to assure you of our safe arrival at Lyme.

"And I thank you for your service to the Order." Elizabeth heaved herself to her feet and curtsied, more or less.

Sir Frederick bowed. Laconia spring-hopped to his side, and they left.

Elizabeth sank back into her rocking chair, stomach roiling, baby kicking, and head pounding. May jumped into her lap, purring and pressing hard against Elizabeth's belly. Between the purring and the rocking, Baby Darcy quieted, though her head and stomach did not.

Brutus appeared from the servants' door—when had he left? "Lady Sage, the weather is fine right now. Would you like to take advantage of it?" The pointed look he gave her suggested there was only one correct answer.

"Fresh air sounds like a fine idea. Shall May accompany us as well?"

Brutus nodded.

15
Chapter

Brutus led them through the narrow, irregular servants' stairs and poorly lit service corridors, insisting she stop to catch her breath often. Finally, they reached a plain wooden door leading into the courtyard in the mews behind the Order offices.

A ten-foot-high red brick fence walled in a garden at least as large as the entire ground floor of the offices. A pair of plain doors along back wall of the offices formed one of the two formal entrances into the garden. A neat stone staircase climbing up from one of the dragon tunnels constituted the other. Espaliered apple trees grew flat against the wall opposite the building, each tree bearing a different apple varietal. Crabapple, dwarf willow and hawthorn trees lined a meandering brick path, creating the illusion of a country garden with beds of flowers—none currently blooming—and shrubs surrounding

them. Stone benches, enhanced with carved bird-type dragons on the supports, dotted the path.

Two whitewashed wooden arbors on the east and west
sides of the courtyard supported naked wisteria vines that
would overflow with vivid purple blooms next year, when
the weather warmed. Fairy dragons would gorge themselves
on the nectar then, all the while listening for any interesting gossip that might come their way as they did. Several
garden wyrms lived among the flowers and trees, tending
the courtyard as effectively as any human gardener. A few
warm-blooded staff pitched in to do what the wyrms could
not, but the garden's management, and all the gossip-worthy
news within, belonged to the wyrms.

Near the arbors, two massive iron-strapped wooden gates
controlled access to the courtyard from the mews. They
could be opened readily from the inside, but from the outside, two separate keys were required. Half a dozen cockatrice guards patrolled the top of the fence, persuading any
outsider who lingered near too long that there was nothing
of interest within the walls. Should that fail, they would
do what was necessary to protect the Order offices. But to
Elizabeth's knowledge, that had never happened.

Sunshine filtered through the naked tree branches, warm-
ing her face as a cool breeze stole the warmth away. How long
had it been since she had been outside? Too long, definitely
too long. Even on the coldest days, she never felt trapped
inside at Pemberley. All she had to do was open the French
doors of the sitting room and take a single step to be in
the garden, tucked in and sleeping for the winter. How she
missed that. "You are right. The weather is quite fine today."

"I am right about many things, Lady Sage." Brutus pointed to a distant spot on the path where Mrs. Sharp walked
alongside a wheeled willow basket pulled by a blue-liveried
drake. He trotted toward them, not even looking over his
shoulder back at Elizabeth.

Surely, he did not suspect the drake of something untoward. Mrs. Sharp was particular about the dragons allowed near Little Anne.

Elizabeth increased her pace, but before she could make it across the courtyard, Brutus had dismissed the liveried drake and took over pulling Little Anne's basket himself. Mrs. Sharp glanced back at Elizabeth, dumbfounded.

"As much as she loves dragons, she is happier with a familiar face." Brutus murmured as Elizabeth reached his side.

She panted harder than she should have at such minor exertion.

Mercy and Truth peeked up out of the basket. "He isss correct."

"Come join usss, May." Truth shimmied toward her sister.

May spring-hopped the rest of the way and flung herself into the basket at Little Anne's feet.

Little Anne giggled and hugged May, who purred and rubbed her face against Anne's chest.

"Such fine weather requires a longer walk." Brutus turned and brought them to the end of the far wall. He turned down the eastern side and pointed to the gate.

This was so out of character for him. Her heart beat harder. Where was he taking them, and why? Brutus had always been loyal, stable, and, most of all, wise. She glanced back at Mrs. Sharp, who raised her brows and shrugged. "Of course, it does. Where shall we go?"

"I know a delightful place to visit." He opened the gate and wheeled Little Anne out.

"Yes, yes! A delightful idea." The zaltys peeked over the edge of the basket, tasting the air with forked tongues.

May stationed herself with paws on the front edge of the basket, tail loose around Anne's wrist. "I love a good visit."

Leave the safety of the Order offices? Had it been only Brutus, she might have balked, but May, Mercy, and Truth as well? What did they know?

Such a pace he kept! Elizabeth could hardly keep up. Mrs. Sharp took her arm, offering much-needed support and encouragement, but neither spoke as they struggled not to lag behind Brutus.

The streets, the path—they were familiar, though. Comfortingly familiar.

Darcy House?

He was taking them home?

A sharp breeze blew dry leaves and hot relief across her shoulders. They were nearly home!

Brutus trotted down the alley leading to the mews, the direction that made the most sense for those warm-bloods subject to the persuasion that May and the zaltys called out: a small pony pulled Little Anne's basket. Brutus stopped at the back door.

Elizabeth scooped Little Anne from the basket and scurried into the house with Mrs. Sharp and the dragons in her wake. The narrow, stone-tiled hall that led to the kitchen sat empty but for them, the stillness safe and embracing.

Elizabeth cradled Little Anne close and leaned hard against the white-painted wall, fighting not to sink to the floor. The warm savory smells from the kitchen, the familiar musk of Amber and Slate, the dry roses kept in dishes through the public rooms swirled in the surrounding air. A cloak of security and peace surrounded her. How could she not have realized how badly she needed this?

"Lady Elizabeth?" Mrs. Davies cried from the end of the servants' hall. "We were not told to expect you!" She rushed toward them.

"Our visit was rather spontaneous." Elizabeth pushed herself away from the wall.

Brutus planted himself in the corridor between Elizabeth and the back door. "They will be staying."

"We will?"

"Yes. You will." He did not bare his teeth, but his tone carried the expression.

"Rally the staff, then, and help Mrs. Sharp prepare the nursery. For now, simply move the cot to the private sitting room off the master suite. I am certain Little Anne needs a nap." She did too, but not yet. Mrs. Sharp took Anne from her. "Brutus, pray come to my office with me."

"May should come, too." He beckoned the tatzelwurm toward them. "And Walker."

"Walker is here?" Why would Walker be in London? What had happened at Pemberley?

"He called to me while on our way here." Something in Brutus' tone implied there was no emergency, at least not yet.

She pressed a hand to her chest, as though it might slow her racing heart. Wishful thinking. "Then, by all means, find him and request that he join us."

Brutus trotted off. Poor Mrs. Davies and Mrs. Sharp looked as bewildered as Elizabeth felt, but they recovered well and surged into action.

Elizabeth and May made their way to the office she and Darcy shared. She fell into the most comfortable chair near the fireplace, currently without a fire, at the far side of the room. Darcy's heavy masculine desk and the dainty feminine one that had once been Lady Anne's stood side by side, pristine as they had been the day their party had left for Pemberley. Traces of Darcy's shaving oil still lingered in the air. Her eyes stung, and she gulped back the feelings she had best contain for now.

Yes, this was home. This was where she needed to be. Whatever Brutus' other reasons might be, he was right. She needed to be here.

May patrolled the room, even climbing out the windows to check the outside for listeners. The cockatrice house guard did an excellent job of keeping small, unannounced dragons away. Why was May being so careful now?

"We have privacy," May climbed back onto the windowsill and licked her shoulder fur.

"Precisely why must you confirm that? Is that strictly necessary?" She scanned the room—yes, over there, the footstool she needed. Was it worth getting up to get it?

Yes. She struggled to her feet to retrieve the dainty embroidered stool.

"Absolutely, Lady Sage." Brutus strode in, Walker winging in behind him. He shut the door.

"I am pleased to see you, Walker, though I confess it all seems so irregular." She settled into her chair and propped up her feet.

"These are most irregular times." Brutus signaled May to shut the windows.

"What brought you here under such unusual circumstances? I understood you were staying in the Order offices for reasons of security." Walker landed on a nearby wooden dragon perch, back-winging to keep it balanced. The lighter perches, made for smaller bird-types, often unbalanced under his weight.

Brutus sat on his haunches, waiting until the last window was shut. "As you are well aware, Lady Sage, the meeting you had with Sir Frederick was not private."

Walker growled softly.

"No, but that is not entirely unexpected, is it?" Elizabeth asked.

"How it was not private is, though." Brutus' tail thumped the carpet near Walker's perch.

"Are you suggesting an organized effort to eavesdrop on my chambers?" Her left hand tightened into a fist.

Walker half-extended his wings, shifting his weight from right to left and back.

"Yes, Lady Sage. May can tell you more about that."

May sat up tall and curled her serpentine tail around her front feet. "When we discovered listeners in the Order offices, I hid in the shadows and eavesdropped on them. They were not the usual gossips. The Council sent them to monitor your meeting."

"Were they dispatched to snoop on Sir Frederick or me?" How dare they! The disrespect, the violation of dominance!

"Does it matter? The Council has made a statement here." Walker snapped his beak in a hard clack.

"I would argue it is important to distinguish which one of us they do not trust," Elizabeth said.

"I beg to differ. Their disrespect alone is problematic. In all likelihood, they distrust both you and Sir Frederick," Walker said.

"That is not all, though." Brutus glanced at May. "There were also listeners sent by the warm-blood members of the Council."

Dragon's bones! "So, their Keepers do not even realize what is going on?" The mind boggled at the implications.

"Apparently." The tip of May's tail flicked. "And, according to what I heard, it does not appear to be an uncommon practice, either."

"I am disappointed. In all of them." Not surprised, to be sure, but it suggested there was a great deal left wanting in the Council's Dragon Keeping.

"It does not end there. I also discovered some sent by other Order officers. The Minister of Keeps, Treasurer, even the Grand Cross of the Pendragon Order," Brutus said.

"Great heavens, was there anyone not trying to listen in on that conversation?" Elizabeth slapped the arms of her chair.

"Many things are happening right now, and few appear to have complete and accurate information readily available."

"What sorts of things? I have not been here long enough to be abreast of it all." Walker glowered, bloodlust in his eyes.

"The matter of Chesil and Cornwall has the Council quite concerned," Elizabeth said.

"Not just that, though." May spring-hopped from the windowsill toward Walker's perch. "The recent discoveries in the Archives—"

"What new findings? April only mentioned a scroll—"

"Since she left, several more articles have been discovered, many of which point to the Order long misrepresenting the role of the minor dragons in the Accords." Elizabeth barely forced the dangerous words out.

Walker flapped and hissed; his perch rocked. "Your father has a hand in this?"

"He and Bede. That's why we are sending her with Sir Frederick to Lyme, where she might continue her work for the Order more safely." Elizabeth pressed the heels of her palms to her temples. "And that does not even take into consideration the issues with Londinium's reign that Drew pointed out to me. I have not had time enough to study those."

"Oh, bloody hell." Walker launched from the dragon perch and landed on the back of Elizabeth's chair, extending his wings protectively. "And all of this happened since April left?"

"It has been an eventful week or so. I had expected her to return by now. What brought you here instead?" Elizabeth covered her mouth with her hand.

"She is well. Do not worry, she is well." Walker laid his serpentine tail over her shoulder.

His demeanor led her to assume it, but words—how she had needed to hear them.

"The escort Brutus sent with her realized they were being followed. He carried her most of the way to Pemberley in his talons. Once they arrived, he and the house guard chased off not one, but three more who had shadowed them from London. Under the circumstances, we deemed it best that I come in her place."

Elizabeth gasped. "Do you think they would have harmed April?"

"I cannot be certain. Most likely, they came to spy on the manor and learn what they could. We could not determine who within the Order offices sent them, but as you noted, it could have been any number of sources. Either way, there was no need to risk Lairda April's safety."

"Of course not." Elizabeth swallowed hard. "I knew the discoveries had the potential to be unsettling, but this far exceeds my expectations."

"That is why I brought you back here," Brutus said. "If the Council's Keepers are not aware of what their dragons are doing, and the rest of the officers are resorting to subterfuge to find out, it is not safe for you at the Order offices any longer."

"By what definition of safe? Dragons, by their nature, are not safe." Given Brutus' glare, she probably should not have said that.

"By the definition for which I was employed, Lady Sage." Brutus bared his fangs, not threateningly—odd to realize there was a non-threatening way to bare one's fangs, but it was so. Here, it was a display to remind them all of the dominance afforded to him by his position.

"I agree." Walker's tail tip flicked against her shoulder. "The information April brought back to us was troubling enough. This even more so. Darcy asked me to convey to you his most polite and fervent desire—"

"Polite and fervent?" Elizabeth looked up at him.

"With all deference to your duty and sound judgement," Walker leaned down until his beak nearly touched her nose. "Darcy and Vicontes wish you to return to Pemberley. Soon."

What better reasons could she have?

"I believe it would be a wise move." Brutus' ears pricked up. "Bede and the material the Historian sent should be on their way with Sir Frederick in the morning. With the level of distrust and chaos amongst the Order's leadership, I would recommend you remove yourself to Pemberley immediately thereafter."

"Historian's materials?" Walker asked with a shrill chirrup.

Elizabeth clutched her forehead. "Bede will need something to keep her occupied while she is away from the main archives. Papa has selected several projects to send with her so that her expertise is not wasted on organizing the Lyme Blue Order office."

"Should I surmise the nature of these materials?"

"It should be obvious," Elizabeth said.

"I do not imagine the Council is aware?"

"No. There is no official catalog of the newest discoveries." Elizabeth hugged Baby Darcy, who kicked and squirmed, probably as dismayed by this discussion as she was. "Drew and Quill Driver will deliver the items into Allister Salt's hands to be packed and transported later this afternoon."

"Someone may follow them here." Walker squawked in Brutus' face.

"I will guide them through little-known passages." Brutus growled back, tail lashing. "I will ensure they and their parcels remain as secure as possible. Still, though, it would be best if you do not return to the offices, Lady Sage. If the Council detects irregularities, things could become complicated."

"I have no choice. They expect a report from me regarding my findings in the old Archives. I cannot beg off." Not that she had any desire to hurry that meeting, or any idea of what she would say.

"Then at least wait until tomorrow, after Sir Frederick and Bede and their cargo have departed. If anything goes wrong with that departure, then you should not go back, regardless. I am sure Walker agrees."

"I do."

"You do not look well. You need to rest." May wove around her legs and purred.

Finally, something she could agree to without reservation. "That is true. I need to lie down and consider all you have said. Brutus, will you oversee the transport of the remainder of the luggage to Darcy House?"

"Immediately, Lady Sage. With your permission, I would recommend that the trunks not be unpacked until after your meeting with the Council, yes?"

16
Chapter

WAS IT A BLESSING or a bad omen that the Council did not summon her that afternoon? Walker, Chisholm, and Brutus all agreed it was a splendid thing. But something niggled at the back of her mind while she took advantage of the time to settle in and, at least temporarily, avoid dealing with cranky dragons. When dealing with the cold-blooded, anything that seemed simple or easy was, invariably, quite the opposite.

Mrs. Davies had the kitchen prepare one of her favorite, albeit simple, meals. Slate and Amber pampered her, which helped relieve her loneliness in April's absence. She slept in her own bed, sound and deep, better than any sleep she had since she had been in London. Who would have thought the change of venue could result in so profound a difference? Only April's presence could improve the situation.

But one could not have everything.

Unless she returned to Pemberley. There she would be near to everything and everyone who brought her joy.

Yes, it might mean shirking her duties to the Order, but each day those duties became harder and harder to perform. More complicated. More ... dangerous. What was she really accomplishing anymore, beyond being some pawn in a conflict she did not fully understand?

There was a discouraging thought if she had ever had one. Maybe that was the point Chisholm and the others had been trying to get her to acknowledge.

Perhaps Papa was right. Her stubbornness was positively draconic.

Little Anne's soft mewling from the adjacent room roused her from her featherbeds. What better way to begin a day?

Somehow between Brutus, Mrs. Sharp, and Mrs. Davies, her rocker had made it back to Darcy House and into the private sitting room she and Darcy cherished. Between the rocker and Anne's cot, she could barely move among the mismatched furniture. The rag rug, fashioned by Lady Anne Darcy, disappeared beneath the clutter, but it was enough to know it was there, a Darcy family legacy, firm and stable. A reminder she most needed.

Elizabeth and Little Anne spent a lovely quarter of an hour rocking, cuddling, and watching May chase her tail, somersaulting and zooming under the furniture like a kitten. Was she entertaining Little Anne, herself, or both?

"Lady Elizabeth," Mrs. Sharp peeked into the sitting room-cum-nursery, her brow furrowed and green eyes troubled.

"Is something wrong?" Elizabeth pushed to her feet, Anne balanced on her hip, her stomach tying itself into preparatory knots.

"I am not really sure." Mrs. Sharp glanced over her shoulder toward the stairs. "But there is a matter downstairs that requires your attention."

"Immediately, I imagine?"

"That would seem best."

"I see." Elizabeth passed Little Anne to her nurse. "What are your plans for the day?"

"We had several calls with minor dragons scheduled, but it may be wise to cancel them. It seems ill-advised to go to the offices to entertain, and Brutus expressed concern about inviting our guests here. Even if he had not, we are not settled enough to properly host anyone today." Mrs. Sharp settled Little Anne on her hip.

"What is the point of having Brutus with us if we do not listen to his advice?" Elizabeth sighed. Listening did not mean she had to like it. "Perhaps arrange for Slate and Amber to have a long visit in the nursery with her. It is high time for them to renew their acquaintance."

"I will see to it."

"And keep to the nursery today. It sounds like things are already becoming tense downstairs."

"Of course, Lady Elizabeth." Mrs. Sharp stepped aside. "I shall have Anne's cot returned to the nursery in time for her nap."

Elizabeth descended the grand staircase, delighting in the smoothness of the wide wooden railing, softness of the carpet, and the knowledge that her destination was only a single short flight away. Sometimes it was the small things that made a difference. Especially when one did not know what waited downstairs.

Mrs. Davies appeared as she reached the bottom step. At Pemberley, Mrs. Reynolds had the same knack of emerging out of nowhere. Come to think of it, so did Mrs. Hill at Longbourn. How did they manage it? "Shall I send tea to your office, Lady Elizabeth?"

So that was where disaster awaited her. "Yes, and some dry toast as well." She swallowed back traces of bile. Not an auspicious flavor upon which to begin the day. "Where is Chisholm?"

"She is waiting for you in your office."

"Excellent." No doubt she was at work to manage the situation. Was that a good thing or a sign that things were already spiraling out of control? Ah well, nothing she could do but find out for herself.

Elizabeth smoothed her skirts, patted her hair, and pulled her shoulders back and spine straight. There was wisdom in entering an unknown company with as many signs of dominance in place as possible. Her heels clicked softly on the polished marble tile, quietly announcing her approach.

The office door had been left open. The annoyed flick of Chisholm's jet-black tail within was apparent from the hall. A rapid twitch like that did not bode well. Lovely.

"Lady Sage! You are come." The relief in Chisholm's voice, what could—

"I have been waiting here for hours, Lady Sage." Bede. Oh, merciful heavens, it was Bede.

Her eerie red eyes seemed to bulge and a red flush along her throat pulsed with her heartbeat. No wonder Chisholm's tail twitched.

"I imagine Bede's complaint to be the first order of business today, yes?" Elizabeth sat down behind Darcy's desk. Chisholm cocked her head, and her forehead wrinkled in a silent question. Elizabeth's feet hardly reached the floor in that chair, and if they did, she could not touch the back. Uncomfortable on the best of days, but it implied an additional show of dominance which dealing with Bede required. For Elizabeth's sake, if not for Bede's.

Chisholm tapped a stack of papers on Elizabeth's desk. "It would appear so, Lady Sage, although there is ample other work to fill the day."

"So then, Bede, since I have other work to attend to, pray explain quickly and succinctly why you are still here. Were you not to have left with Sir Frederick for Lyme by now?"

Bede's black and white speckled hide glistened like glass beads in the sunbeam where she stood, savoring the warmth. Her tail lashed along the carpet, scales catching with a sound like dry leaves rustling in the wind. Her toes flexed and the red patch on her throat swelled. "Yes, Lady Sage. I was supposed to go. You realize the Historian disapproved of my departure, but Drew and Quill Driver insisted I come here, and Axel has not left me alone for a moment." She glanced over her shoulder at the far corner where the tip of Axel's brown brindle nose was visible through the peeked-open servants' door. "Am I in confinement? To be treated like a prisoner?"

Too distracted to answer the question. Not unusual, but her general twitchiness suggested something more.

"I explained to you why you were here. More than once." Chisholm snarled, her tail thumping against the carpet. "As for the Sage's question—"

Elizabeth drummed her fingers along the edge of the desk. "You would do well to remember you would be in mortal danger staying at the office. It is in not only in your best interest, but that of the Historian's and the Scribe's offices, that you remain capable of doing your work for them."

"But I do not understand how I am to do my tasks here, and not in the Archives." Bede shifted her weight right and left. Was that her way of subduing the urge to stomp?

"Now is not the time to pursue those tasks. Now is the time to wait and follow orders. Once you settle into your new situation, you will return to your assignments."

"And what am I to work on? All the necessary—"

Elizabeth pressed her elbows against the desk and pulled herself up taller. It might not leave an impression on Bede, but it helped her. "You need not be aware of the details—"

"I have to know what you plan. You must tell me." Bede sucked in a chest-inflating breath.

Elizabeth rose to her feet. "No. You have proven that you lack the ability to keep information to yourself. So, for now, you must trust me."

"It is necessary for me to understand what is going to happen to me." Bede deflated and paced the length of the office, toward the fireplace and back, worrying her front paws. "I cannot think, I cannot eat, I cannot sleep not knowing."

That would explain her frantic state.

Chisholm's upper lip curled, a typical reaction for any dragon to such a demonstration of weakness.

"I understand it is uncomfortable. But there is nothing to be done for it now. The nature of the situation is too sensitive to risk the inadvertent slip of a tongue."

"Are you saying I cannot be trusted?" Bede flushed redder and the traces of her scent-defense wafted from her.

Elizabeth pressed her hand to her ribs and swallowed the urge to gag. "You will mind your tongue, control your defenses, and be careful of the accusations you are making. I am well within my purview as Dragon Sage to manage this matter. I am trying to preserve your hide. If you cannot appreciate that and cooperate with me, I will order you taken into custody and detained as a threat to the Order because of the information you possess."

Bede skittered back, halfway across the room. "Information? I have no information!"

"And therein lies the problem. You have no concept of what you know and what danger is inherent in it. You can either tolerate the gentle care we are providing for you, or I can instruct Brutus to chain you in the cellar until you might be transported where you can do no harm. For now, I will leave you the choice, but I will not hesitate to decide for you the moment you fight me." Where she would acquire chains was not apparent, but if needs must, then she would manage. Mrs. Davies was incredibly resourceful.

"But I was to have gone by now. Why am I still here?" Pray Bede would not continue to whine so, or poor Chisholm might actually slap her.

"That is an excellent question and, as I recall, the starting place for this conversation. I had hoped you would give me an answer—"

"This letter that was delivered by Laconia last night might explain." Chisholm pulled a sealed missive from a pile on the desk.

"Why was I not informed?" Elizabeth struggled to keep her voice level.

"You were already asleep when it arrived. Mrs. Davies threatened to skin us all if we woke you for anything less than the start of a dragon war."

Mrs. Davies could be formidable that way, but little did she know that a late-night missive might actually herald disaster. Elizabeth pressed her eyes with thumb and forefinger. "Give me the letter."

"I did not open it, as it bears the seal of confidentiality." Chisholm pointed to the blue wax seal with a spot of black in the center. "I have never seen one of those before. I thought it was a rumor to keep secretaries observant."

"Neither have I." In fact, Elizabeth had never even heard of it. She took the message from Chisholm's paw, and Chisholm stepped away from the desk, glowering at Bede lest she shift toward them and catch a glimpse of the letter.

The double wax seal proved stubborn, tearing through the outer page as she struggled to remove it. Sir Frederick—who else would have sent a message via Laconia?—must have expected that, as a blank page enclosed the actual missive.

Lady Elizabeth,

I am unavoidably delayed in my departure for Land's End. The Council has detained me while a new document is prepared for delivery to Cornwall.

Of course, as only the messenger, I am not privy to whose pen composes the document or what it will contain. I am sure you will hear a great deal of gossip on the matter, though.

I have no idea when to expect our departure, but I will inform you as soon as I receive my orders.

Yours,

FW.

Blast and bloody dragon's bones! Elizabeth folded the note and tucked it into her sleeve. Into a locked box it would go at the earliest possible convenience. "Sir Frederick has been unavoidably delayed."

"I am not surprised." Bede snorted and scratched at the carpet. "That is exactly what I expected."

"Explain. How is it you are privy to such things?" Chisholm's narrowed eyes challenged Bede as effectively as a growl.

"When one hears as much gossip as I do, then one learns to put things together to reach useful conclusions." Bede puffed up and stepped toward Chisholm.

"And one can never be certain if her conclusions are correct until they are put to the test." Elizabeth marched around to the front of the desk and bared her teeth enough that Bede caught the gesture. "What have you heard? Allow me to draw my own conclusions."

"Yes, of course, Lady Sage." Bede deflated and bowed her head. "The general assumption is that the matter of Cornwall has roused Buckingham—that is, Londinium—from his lethargy."

"Indeed, that is most interesting." Was Elizabeth the only one not aware of the gossip about the Brenin? "Why is that the assumption?"

"Londinium is known for spending a great deal of time asleep. Recently, his attendants have been quite busy acquiring significant quantities of food. Other things too, but the food is the most notable."

"Londinium is eating again?"

"Not merely eating, Lady Sage, but eating as though coming out of hibernation." Bede clenched her front paws together and held them before her chest.

That could not be a good thing. Elizabeth's throat burned and her stomach turned over. Where was that dry toast? "Is there any sign of what precipitated this change?"

"That is less clear. Some suggest Chesil, some suggest Matlock, some suggest ... suggest he is concerned about the Archives."

"Chesil is a part of the gossip? What are they saying about Chesil?" Elizabeth leaned back against the bulky desk.

"That there is a huge sea dragon at Lyme that tried to eat Sir Frederick and is bigger than any Blue Order dragon." Bede blinked rapidly as she mimicked the dragon who had spread the news.

"Where did that information come from?"

"Cockatrice observed the whole thing. And fairy dragons, and rock wyrms on the cliffs. The whole affair was in no way private. I cannot believe any warm-blood would think such a thing. Do not your kind realize there are dragons observing everything?"

Dragon's bones! They had all been fooling themselves with wishful thinking. "Why would Matlock be a concern for Londinium?"

"You mean Grand Dug Matlock?" Bede had the audacity to roll her eyes. Impertinent creature! "They have never gotten along, and it has only gotten worse as Londinium has grown fat and idle while Matlock was named to a title of greater authority than Cornwall."

"I see." Actually, she did not, though she should have, and would need to give it a great deal more thought. She pinched her temples. "Should I expect Londinium has also gotten wind of the specifics of what you found in the Archives?"

"No. The Historian has been quite diligent about that. No, I believe Londinium already has some knowledge about what was secreted away, which is an interesting notion in itself, you see—"

Elizabeth raised an open hand. "Yes, I can well imagine. I am interested, though, in why you did not name Cornwall among Londinium's concerns, or do you class him with the issues of Chesil?"

"Londinium has considered Cornwall a great mistake for a very long time. The topic is not discussed because it brings down the Brenin's fury on whoever mentions it."

"Indeed?" How could she have not been aware? Did no one mention it simply because they expected her to already be the repository of all common knowledge?

"So, there is a dragon-kept secret, after all, and it is one of our best-known unmentionables. Imagine that. The Dragon Sage in the dark!" Bede laughed, a coarse, barking, incredibly unpleasant sound that rasped sparks on Elizabeth's temper like a blacksmith's file. "There was a time when Cornwall was the next most dominant dragon to Londinium, and so named heir. No one expected him to become what he is now. Such an embarrassment to Londinium."

Dragon's spit and fire! That cast an entirely different light on April's concerns about Matlock.

"Just because Cornwall is not one of the core issues rousing Londinium does not mean he is not upset about it. Londinium is, in fact, quite angry about how much worse Cornwall has become, especially since the whole kerfuffle with Kellynch. And he puts much of the blame on you." Bede caught Elizabeth's gaze.

Elizabeth shuddered. "How is it my fault?"

"You opposed Cornwall in his case against Kellynch," Chisolm whispered. "That blow to his dominance damaged his reputation in the kingdom. What more would a major dragon need to trigger bad behavior?"

"To be sure, except for Londinium's tail-lickers, there are none who believe it to be your fault. Not that one of them might not try to gain favor with Londinium by—"

"That is enough. We do not need to hear more." Chisholm snarled until Bede skittered back. "Is Brutus aware of the situation?"

Bede's forehead wrinkled and she blinked rapidly. "Come to think of it, he asked me several questions yesterday that suggested that he might be. He can be quite clever about some matters. Maybe that is why he secreted you away from the Order offices yesterday. It seems the sort of thing he might do."

"As a matter of fact, it was." Axel pushed the servants' door open and slipped through. "There has been no specific threat made, Lady Sage. No individual that he is aware of who is likely to present a danger. But word of the Brenin's agitation was enough for him to act to improve your safety by bringing you to Darcy House."

Elizabeth bit her upper lip and drew a deep breath. Holding her breath did not provide instant patience, but at least it kept her from hasty words. "And when was I to be informed of the situation?"

"When there was something concrete to share with you. Sometimes it is critical to follow one's instincts and sort out the whys of it later. Brutus' reputation for excellent instincts is why he was assigned to you."

"I wish I had such instincts," Bede muttered.

Axel was right, not that Elizabeth liked it at the moment. "I am grateful to have them exercised on my behalf. As should you also be, Bede. Follow my example, and do as you have been asked. Sometimes it is crucial to take the advice of a more expert dragon."

"Yes, Lady Sage."

Chapter 17

ONE MIGHT EXPECT BEDE'S acquiescence would have ended the discussion, but one would have been wrong. Mind-numbingly wrong.

After another half hour of questions, repetitions, and subjects entirely unrelated, Axel all but dragged Bede from Darcy's office to the Darcy House library. For generations, the Darcys had been avid conservators of Blue Order material, though they had been more interested in its acquisition and preservation than in cataloging those items. They still lacked a comprehensive listing of the rare tomes on the history of the Blue Order that lay tucked among other volumes, both at Pemberley and at Darcy House.

Elizabeth closed her eyes and leaned back in Darcy's much-too-big-for-her leather desk chair. If she breathed deep and concentrated, she could detect his scent on the leather. Heavens, how she needed that support, that stability right now.

She had not exaggerated the importance of combing through the library and searching for clues, in those as-yet not cataloged volumes, to shed light on the situation with Londinium. Gracious, he had been reigning as Brenin for over two hundred years at this point, and still no one really had a solid understanding of his reign. What might Bede turn up? Her knees trembled and insides quaked.

Why had she never considered the need to understand the dragon king before? Out of sight, out of mind was the best, if unsatisfying, answer. She had barely interacted with him, aside from a brief, uneventful presentation when she received the title of Sage. From there, she had been encouraged to assume him indolent and ineffective and that the real power lay with the Council.

How naïve to believe that.

Naïve to believe so many things. She wrapped her arms around her middle, trying to gather up the pieces of her world. Intrigues and secrets abounded in the Order exactly as they did in the Royal Court, with as much potential for damage. Why did that seem so surprising?

Where was the truth? Whom could she trust? How was any of that to be established?

Who were those out to impress Londinium, and how far would they go in the quest for his favor? Yes, those were the most pertinent questions right now.

Brutus, she needed to talk to Brutus.

"Lady Sage?" She jumped at Chisholm's soft voice near her elbow.

"Would I be wrong to expect you need to speak to Brutus and perhaps Walker? I will fetch them, if you like." Chisholm gazed up at her, sparkling jet eyes full of understanding and concern.

"Was I so obvious?"

Chisholm shrugged and scurried for the servants' door to the service corridors. Not that she needed to remain out of sight in the house, but those pathways permitted her to move more rapidly. Dragons running through the public halls made the staff nervous. With excellent reason, to be sure, but now was not the time to spread unnecessary alarm.

Exactly how much alarm did the circumstances warrant? With any luck, Brutus could shed some light on the matter.

Baby Darcy kicked and wriggled, forcing her from Darcy's chair. Perhaps a bit of walking would settle him. The wee one was so sensitive to her moods, more so than Anne was. Or so it seemed with all the restless movement.

She reached the fireplace opposite Darcy's desk and turned back to cross the morning sunbeams striping the office's length once again. Dragon's breath, she was tired. So, so tired. Would she ever feel rested and strong again?

Brutus and Walker appeared at the green-baize service door.

Elizabeth stopped at the wing chairs near the fire. These were not dragons to whom she needed to give reminders of dominance. She dropped like a flour sack into the nearest chair. "Walker, I imagine Brutus has filled you in on the details of the situation?" No point in trying to hide the annoyance in her voice. They could smell it on her, even if her tone and posture did not give it away.

"Such as there are, yes, he has." Walker landed on the heavy iron dragon perch that had been brought in for him near the fireplace, back-winging to keep it balanced as he settled his weight on it. "And I agree with his assessment of the situation. It is unlikely any of the major dragons would take action against you, but minor dragons are far more difficult to predict, especially the ones trying to curry favor."

"Londinium's reputation for generous favors, doled out to those who anticipate his intentions and act on them, makes for a dangerous and unpredictable situation. It allows him to deny any complicity in their actions to the Council. Even though they are all aware of the truth." Brutus stationed himself next to the perch, sitting on his haunches. Interesting choice of position. He signaled not only solidarity, but recognition of Walker's dominance and that he would work under Walker's command.

The last thing Elizabeth needed was for those two to be at odds.

"But those who guess wrong pay a high price." Walker's lashing black serpentine tail made clear his opinion on that fact. "Only dragons of a particular disposition get involved in playing such games."

"Would you consider them bold or stupid?" Brutus looked up at Walker.

"A bit of both, and particularly dangerous. It is best to stay well out of their reach until their threat is neutralized."

"Is that to say someone is assigned to the task?" That was the sort of question one had to ask, but did not necessarily want to know the answer.

"Not officially." Walker shifted his weight from side to side. "But Londinium is not the only dragon with whom one might curry favor. Matlock has his own tail-lickers who would readily do the job for him."

If both of them had minor dragons working under them, without specific direction, with just the assumption they would do the right things? Dragon's blood, breath, and bones! Who was running matters in the Order?

"And since Matlock needs the Dragon Sage, his tail-lickers are unlikely to raise a talon against you." Brutus slapped the carpet with his tail, narrowly missing the base of the perch.

"That is some relief, I suppose." A very little relief when one considered the dangers that had just been laid out.

"If I may be so bold as to suggest that neither you nor Bede answer any summons to the Order offices that Walker or I have not vetted first."

"And arranged the security for said meeting," Walker added.

"I can readily see the danger Bede could be in, but do you believe they would act against a warm-blooded Order officer?" Had she been a fool for trusting that the rules against harming warm-bloods would keep her safe?

"It is not a chance we are willing to take." Brutus drummed his front feet and looked at Walker, who nodded.

Elizabeth slumped back in the wing chair. Every instinct, every inch of her being, longed to argue, to prove there was some order left in her world. But to what point? Only to delude herself. Nothing would alter what they knew to be true. "I suppose you will make Darcy aware of the situation?"

"He already suspects a great deal." Walker's squawk suggested Darcy was not happy about it either.

Mr. Davies' distinct knock sounded on the door. "Lady Elizabeth, you have a caller."

She clutched her forehead. "Tell them I am not receiving any calls today."

"Forgive me, madam, but the caller is not at the front door, but in the cellar."

"Then she is definitely not receiving callers." Brutus stood and snarled.

"I do not think the Barwines will be moved, madam."

Elizabeth gasped and clutched the arms of her chair. "Barwines Chudleigh is in the cellar? Is she alone?"

"As I understand, she is the only member of the Council who can enter through the dragon tunnels from the Order offices. The entryway was insufficient for Old Pemberley in his later years, and the vicontes has had no need for alterations, yet."

That was a comfort. One annoyed Council dragon would be quite enough company. Given their scowls, neither Brutus nor Walker shared in her relief.

"Then I must go to the Barwines. Alone." If Chudleigh had come all this way, at considerable inconvenience to herself, it was definitely not to meet with anyone of a lesser status. "Warn May that she is not to eavesdrop on our conversation, and I trust all of you to respect the need for privacy, as well."

Brutus bristled at the implication but lowered his chin to the ground. "Yes, Lady Sage."

Walker merely glowered.

Chudleigh's distinct floral dragon musk filtered up the cold, dim cellar stairs, reaching Elizabeth well before the light from her candle extended down to the waiting amphithere. The wooden steps creaked and squealed under her slow, deliberate steps, as much a matter of dignity as they were of safety. Musty dampness emphasized the dangerous irregularity of the encounter.

Was it her imagination, or did she really feel the chill of the cellar floor through her shoes? Even if it were only her imagination, the unpleasant sensation intensified her desire to be anywhere else.

But she was here and needed to act in her role. So, she lit half a dozen candles in simple pewter sconces along the two walls adjacent to the stairs, then turned to greet Barwines Chudleigh.

Chudleigh waited in the middle of the cellar, amidst barrels and boxes and trunks, balanced over her coiled tail, lustrous feathered wings spread. Her spectacular multicolored head-feathers brushed the ceiling, catching in the dust and cobwebs there, her need to display dominance overriding her vanity. Chudleigh despised dust in her head feathers.

"You will forgive me for my abbreviated greeting," Elizabeth braced along the wall as she fought to rise from bended knees.

Chudleigh's long, forked tongue flicked the air. Was she tasting the air for traces of uninvited dragons? "So, you choossse to accept my call."

As though there had been an option. "One does not turn away a Barwines when she honors your home with a call."

"Why have you fled the Order officessss?" Draconic directness at its finest.

"Fled is a strong word."

"Your security head brought you out with no preparation or warning. That seemssss like fleeing." Chudleigh leaned a little closer, tongue flicking. "It is the act of prey and is unseemly for one of your sssstation."

Was that her concern? She had a point, though. "So is ignoring a genuine threat, especially when one is in my condition. Protecting one's young is not the action of prey." She pressed a hand to her belly.

Chudleigh's head bobbed as she pulled back. "Allowancessss must be made for such reasons. Still, though, none of that changes the need for us to understand what you found in the Archivessss."

Why did it always go back to the Archives? "We found the amphithere paintings you suspected. They are being cleaned and will be sent to you as soon as they are properly documented. You might find them helpful to your purposes."

"Issss that all you found?"

"What has you so concerned? There is more than what you have told me."

Chudlcigh pulled back, wings open and upraised, like the hood of a cobra ready to strike. "You have been told all you need to know."

"We have fulfilled your request. What more is there to be said?"

"Do not be impertinent, Ssssage." The statement ended with an angry hiss.

"Do not treat me with the respect given to a fairy dragon."

"An impertinent fairy dragon issss eaten."

"Are you threatening me?" Elizabeth leaned into her heels and flared her elbows.

Chudleigh folded her wings neatly across her back. "No, I am not, nor would I. I would never engage in ssssuch a brutish action."

"No one on the Council has been behaving according to their usual standards of decorum during my stay here."

"These are difficult dayssss. "

Elizabeth chewed her lower lip. Time to be very careful. "I have some small and incomplete understanding of the difficulties."

"You do?"

"Londinium, Cornwall, Chesil, Matlock ... some small awareness." Perhaps it was best not to go on.

Chudleigh stared into her eyes, searching, studying, considering. Though every human instinct demanded that she flinch, run, hide from the penetrating gaze, Elizabeth stood firm and stared back. "Then you understand that opening up additional areassss of ... difficulty... right now will only inflame issuessss further."

"Is that to say you want to make them go away?"

"That would be for the besssst."

Carefully. She had to tread carefully. "There are many ways for that to happen, some more permanent than others."

"You sssspeak the truth."

Elizabeth's voice dropped to a hoarse whisper. "Some I can tolerate, but some I cannot."

Chudleigh rocked back and forth, tongue darting in and out just past her fangs. "It is unwise to try to permanently remove issuessss. They have a way of rising up anew, like a phoenix from the flames."

"An apt analogy, Barwines."

"Sometimes a truth is best held until there are ears available to hear it. And," she tapped her tail tip hard on the floor, "there is wisdom in being able to identify the time to allow a bigger dragon to handle matterssss."

Not the first time Chudleigh had offered that sound advice. "And you believe this is one of those times?"

"Do not lose faith in bigger dragonssss."

"Even when they are angry and unreasonable?"

"You are very familiar with them. Consider what sssort of situation would render them so. Perhapsss, you have not contemplated that perspective?"

Ouch! Elizabeth winced. "The Barwines makes an excellent point."

"Of courssse, I do."

"What do bigger dragons require in order to handle matters?"

"Time and space in which to prioritize the issuessss before them."

Not wholly unreasonable. "What does that look like?"

"You have already begun by removing Bede from the Archivessss. Your instincts are sound. You should follow them."

"I see."

"Good. Then I will leave you now." Chudleigh turned away and slithered toward the tunnels. "This conversssation never happened."

"Pray, allow me one question before you leave."

Chudleigh looked over her wing at Elizabeth. "It dependssss on the question."

"Brutus fears those seeking favor with Londinium."

"Not unwissse."

"Should we fear those seeking favor with Matlock?"

"Can Matlock risk Pemberley'ssss wrath?" Chudleigh disappeared into the darkness.

Elizabeth sank onto the bottom step.

What had little Pemberley to do with any of this? Surely, she was not aware of the intrigues. But then again, Chudleigh had not implied that she was. Merely that Matlock could not afford to alienate her.

Pemberley might be young now, but she would grow up. When she did, she would be the major dragon nearest to his territory. And as a vicontes, she stood every chance of becoming an officer of the Order, even a part of the Council herself. As young as she was, she had already gained unprecedented popularity among the local minor dragons, and many of the smaller major dragons. If Pemberley turned against Matlock, significant repercussions could ensue.

Did that mean she could trust Matlock? It seemed like Chudleigh did, at least enough to recommend that Elizabeth allow bigger dragons to handle matters.

Clearly, though, London was not safe for her, for Little Anne, or Baby Darcy.

Dragon's bones!

They were not the only ones at risk. Papa and Lady Astrid, both of whom well knew what was in the Archives, were in almost as much danger. And that was something a dragon her size could—should—handle.

18
Chapter

THE NEXT MORNING, LACONIA met Elizabeth with another message from Sir Frederick. Still without orders for their departure, it was their opinion that it might be several more days yet before that happened. Not surprising, but it was inconvenient.

Inconvenient, like the piles of work that had gathered on her desk waiting for attention, driving her to the parlor to avoid the reminders. Inconvenient, like the growing list of questions to which she had no firm answers. Inconvenient, like the uncertainty that dogged her.

Enough of that.

Brutus' and Walker's concerns aside, the delay would have been tolerable except that Bede had grown bored with the tasks in the Darcy House library and would soon require more engaging employment. Which naturally would not be available to her. Not here.

The household did not need to manage Bede's boredom on top of everything else.

How was she so efficient at processing so much information? Single-mindedness helped, no doubt, but even so, her acumen was remarkable.

Elizabeth scanned the parlor. Maybe among the decorative artifacts on the shelves there might be something worthy of Bede's efforts. But no, nothing that important was kept in a public room. Her now-cold teacup caught her eye. It still smelled appetizing, though. Perhaps that would help settle her stomach.

If only Bede could also write, then there would be many tasks which she could take on. But her penmanship still required a codebreaker to understand, and she hated the task with a passion. No benefit would come of having her commit anything to paper. What else—

Brutus slipped in from the servants' door. "The Historian and the Scribe will arrive shortly. The carriage left the Order offices a quarter of an hour ago."

Best get that disagreeable conversation over with soon.

Brutus sat on his haunches beside her. "I am concerned about the news Laconia brought. It is alarming and unusual that a dragon like Londinium would take so long to craft a missive. I interpret that to mean there is something he is waiting for—and I do not trust that such a thing will be in your best interest ... or Matlock's. But Matlock has his own security team to manage his affairs."

"Is that your way of saying you want me to remove from London?" In a strange way, his lack of directness suggested the urgency of his desire, avoiding the openness which sometimes got a warm-blood's back up.

"As soon as possible. I have heard nothing specific, but my scales are itching, and it is not scale mites. There are several larger minor dragons who are eager to curry Londinium's favor. Ambition, in warm- or cold-blooded forms, is not to be trusted." His tail scraped against the carpet as it lashed.

"Even if I did not agree with you, I am ready to be done with London."

Brutus' ears pricked. "When?"

"As soon as the matter of Bede is settled, I will depart."

"You should not wait on her account."

"I realize she has offended you on more than one occasion, but you must trust me. She cannot be left to find her own way through this. She is as valuable as she is unable to protect herself. Consider her protection part of your charge now."

"I would rather not." Brutus' upper lip drew back to expose his upper fangs.

"It is what I need from you."

"I understand, Lady Sage." He grumbled under his breath but dipped his head, a sure sign that he would acquiesce.

A knock sounded on the door, and Mr. Davies' voice announced, "Lady Astrid and Mr. Bennet to see you, Lady Elizabeth. Are you in?"

That always seemed such a duplicitous question, given that, if she were not present, the question could not be asked. Ah, warm-blooded conventions ... "Show them to my office."

"Not the parlor or the drawing room?"

"No, and do not bring tea, at least not until I call for it." A meeting of business, particularly one with Papa present, should be conducted as if one meant business.

"Shall I attend?" Brutus asked.

"I want you there, but first, bring Chisholm to join us. I may need both of you to support my assertions."

"Right away." Brutus scurried off.

Elizabeth pushed herself up from her chair and smoothed her dress over her bulging middle. "Be calm, little one, we shall be home soon." If only she could take her own advice.

At least it was true. They would be home soon.

Mr. Davies opened the office door. "Lady Astrid and Mr. Bennet." It seemed odd to introduce people she knew so well, but apparently Mr. Davies perceived the need for the formality. Such a treasure, both him and his wife.

Elizabeth stood behind her desk. There was no need to go so far as to employ the dominance of Darcy's furniture today. The wing chairs near the fireplace would have been more comfortable for all involved, but a little discomfort would establish her point more effectively. At least that was her theory.

Papa hobbled in, leaning more heavily on his walking stick than ever. His hair was mussed, like he had been worrying his fingers through it, and his coat was frowsy. Had his housekeeper not attended to it—or had he kept her from doing so? Ink and dust stained his gnarled fingers—how much work had he been doing? Had he even been back to Middleset House recently? No point in asking if he was eating properly.

Lady Astrid stood beside him, her dark-blue gown and matching wool pelisse smart and neat as always. But there were shadows in her eyes behind her glasses, and dark circles beneath them. Lines creased the sides of her mouth, the effects of too many frowns and too little laughter. Had they been there the last time Elizabeth had seen her?

"Lady Astrid, Papa, thank you for coming on such short notice. Pray sit down." Elizabeth gestured to the chairs near her desk.

Papa shambled to the nearest seat and dropped into it. "This is all most irregular, Lizzy. I insist on knowing what all this is about. Of all people, you should understand there is work to be done, and, I fear, little time in which to do it."

What fresh disaster dawned today? "What do you mean, little time?"

Lady Astrid perched on the chair closest to Elizabeth's desk. "Not an hour ago, one of the Council secretary dragons burst in on us and announced that the Archive wing had been found unstable and, as of this evening, no one would be permitted into those rooms until the structural issues are addressed."

Papa rapped his walking stick on the floor. "That is utter poppycock. Drew and Quill Driver have assured me of the soundness of those tunnels. I told the secretary to inform the Council of that—"

"I am troubled to hear—"

"As you should be. I insist you must speak on our behalf. Tell the Council they are being ridiculous. Those tunnels are safe, as you have seen for yourself. Have Brutus tell them. He is charged with looking after you, and he did not identify danger there."

"I hate to contradict the Council, but the Historian is right." Lady Astrid adjusted her glasses. "It is a terrible hardship for us to be turned away from our work. Even if we no longer have access to the most intriguing of those documents," a deep frown creased her forehead, "there is plenty of other work to accomplish. We have not gotten those paintings to Barwines Chudleigh yet, for example."

"That will need to be done today." Elizabeth smoothed back a few stray locks.

"Whatever for? What place has she to disrupt the more significant—"

Brutus and Chisholm slipped in through the service door, Walker swooping in on their heels.

"What is he doing here?" Papa glowered at Walker as though he were some harbinger of doom.

"You have checked to ensure privacy?" Elizabeth asked.

"Yes, Lady Sage." Brutus and Chisholm dipped their chins to the floor. How quick they were to pick up on Papa's attitude with a quick reminder of who they considered dominant in the room.

"Privacy? What is going on?" Papa's face flushed.

"Far more than you realize." Walker landed on the desk, flapping his leathery black wings near Papa's nose.

"What have you done now, Lizzy? I knew your outspoken ways would push the Council past their breaking point. You have angered them, have you not? And now they are taking it out on us to punish you. This is intolerable. I insist you go back there and sort this out. I hope you have learned—"

"Pipe down, you old fool." Walker fully extended his wings and blocked Papa's line of sight to Elizabeth. "You have no idea what you are talking about."

Papa skidded his chair back. "She has been in regular meetings with them and their temperament has grown worse and worse with each one."

"And you assume that is the reason for their ire? I expected you could reason better than a child." Walker knocked a book off the desk with his whipping tail.

Lady Astrid laid her fingertips on the arm of Papa's chair. "Perhaps you should hear them out. It sounds like matters are more complex than we realized."

"Oh, very well. Have your share in the conversation." Papa rolled his eyes. So much like one of Mama's expressions, Elizabeth tried not to laugh.

But this was no laughing matter. "To keep a complicated issue as brief as I can, the Council faces several critical issues right now. While the discoveries you are making in the Archives are significant, they stand to be a dangerous distraction from their greatest concerns."

"What can be more important than shedding new light on the Pendragon Accords?" Papa slammed his hands on the desk, near Walker, who barely restrained his attack reflex to peck at his hands.

One deep breath. Two. Three. "Making sure that the Blue Order remains intact to exercise them."

All the color drained from Lady Astrid's already-pale face, and she gripped the edge of Elizabeth's desk. "Dragon's fire! What is going on?"

"And what would you understand of such things? What manner of nefarious dealings are you involved with, Lizzy?"

"Take care with the accusations you make toward the Sage." Chisholm stepped up beside Elizabeth, nostrils flaring and eyes wide. "You believe that the Council is forthcoming about what is going on? You cannot be so naïve."

"Where do you get such privileged information, then?"

"There is a tremendous amount of gossip, of course." Chisholm's clipped tones implied she would rather bite than explain.

"How can you bother with gossip? You know there is little truth to it." Papa would do well not to challenge Chisholm so.

"Every minor dragon who wants to survive pays attention to it." Brutus snapped his jaws.

"One has to understand how to use it." Chisholm edged a little closer to Elizabeth. So protective. "One never takes a single source seriously but looks for commonalities and patterns among various sources. From there, one can build information. Not unlike what you do with the histories."

"And what intelligence have you been building?" Lady Astrid looked aside, as though dreading the answer.

"In short, that Londinium's grasp on dominance is slipping, and the possibility that Cornwall could step in as Brenin could usher in the downfall of the Order as a whole."

Lady Astrid gasped while Papa snorted. "This is why gossip must be ignored. Snippets of information get taken out of context, blown out of proportion, until minor dragons like you are running about spreading needless alarm. I cannot believe you would pay attention to such nonsense."

"It is not needless alarm." Walker's tail nearly knocked the inkstand off the desk.

"You too, Walker? You are such a steady fellow, I thought—"

"Stop your yammering and listen!" He hissed in Papa's face, wings spread and tail straight out behind him. "Chisholm's information is accurate, and Brutus can corroborate everything she is saying. As can I. Matters are precarious right now."

"Which renders our research into the Accords—"

"Dangerous and possibly deadly." Brutus' abrupt words chilled the room.

"What?" Lady Astrid squeezed her eyes shut and shook her head. "We are academics, not politicians."

"Academics who are looking for information that could disrupt the ambitions of the politically-minded," Chisholm said. "Neither Londinium nor Cornwall is interested in the issues of minor dragons, and if Matlock is, he has not the attention to spare for them now."

"But that is not the worst of it." Brutus glanced at Chisholm.

"What else concerns you?" Lady Astrid whispered.

"How convenient it would be to have your efforts silenced." Brutus let those words hang in the air.

"The Accords outlaw such an action." Papa huffed and folded his arms over his chest, hinting that he might be done with this conversation.

"Yes, they do. They forbid a great number of things which happen on a daily basis." Elizabeth struggled more than she should have to keep her voice soft and level.

"The major dragons would not dare such a crime against the Accords."

"They are not the only dangerous dragons in the Blue Order." Brutus bared his teeth and hissed in Papa's face.

Papa gasped and jumped, nearly tipping his chair over backward. "Was that a threat?"

"No, a demonstration that threats can come from sources you dismiss as harmless."

"You believe there is a credible threat?" Lady Astrid caught Elizabeth's gaze.

"We will repair to Pemberley soon."

Brittle, dangerous silence hung in the air, threatening to shatter into dangerous shards.

"When I let Crosswoods, my property in Shropshire, I retained the use of the dower house there," Lady Astrid stared at her hands. "It will not take me long to close the house here. I will endeavor to depart when you do."

"If I may?" Chisholm glanced at Elizabeth for permission. "Considering that it is impossible to predict what will happen while you are away, it might be wise to identify the most valuable remaining documents and take them with you for safekeeping in the interim."

"Perhaps under the guise of retrieving those paintings for Barwines Chudleigh before you are forbidden access to the Archives," Elizabeth suggested.

"Yes, yes, that is a good idea. Perhaps Drew and Quill Driver can help with that. I am sure my Friend Bylock will assist as well. Are he and Verona in danger, too?"

"It is impossible to say. But if they have heard of or seen the same documents you have …" Chisholm allowed her voice to trail off, saying much by not saying anything at all.

"I shall invite Quill Driver to the dower house with me, as well."

"How many of the remaining documents can you take with you?" Elizabeth asked.

"No more than half, I fear. My coach is not spacious, and I would not put such valuable documents on a luggage cart."

"I will remain and protect what is left." Papa struggled to stand.

"Do not be ridiculous." Walker squawked. "You can barely walk. How can you protect yourself against nefarious dragons?"

Brutus sneered. "You need protection; you cannot offer it."

"Do not be impertinent with me."

"He is right," Elizabeth whispered.

Papa leaned heavily on his walking stick, teetering slightly, and shook his head. "I cannot. I will not go back to Longbourn."

Of course, he could not. Not after he had been removed as Keeper there. Even with all of Mr. Collins' improvements, Papa could hardly live with a man who did not hear dragons, yet played the role of the master of a dragon estate.

"Naturally, that is not an option." Elizabeth bit her lower lip and sighed. "You will come to Pemberley with me. We will bring the remaining documents with us, and you can have the use of the library there. Even if you cannot translate the documents we bring, there is plenty of productive work to be done in the library—"

"No. I insist Bede must come with me." He pulled himself up as straight as he could and expanded his chest. Face-saving, just like a dragon. "With her and Drew, we will be able to continue the work we have begun, so that when this other political nonsense is over, we will be able to present useful findings to whoever is left to present them to."

Papa and Bede? One of them was difficult, but the two together would be enough to drive her, much less Darcy, mad.

Walker chirruped. "What he says makes sense." Given his impatience with both Papa and Bede, the statement was difficult to ignore.

"Considering the delays Sir Frederick is experiencing, it might be better to remove Bede from London as soon as possible." Chisholm did not appear to like the suggestion any better than Elizabeth did. "She has finished her work in the Darcy House library."

"If Bede can accompany me, I will go to Pemberley. Otherwise, I must stay here." Stubbornness settled into the lines on Papa's face.

Obstinate, prideful man, acting as if he was doing her some favor in allowing her to save his life.

"I will take word to Pemberley immediately and return to accompany you when you leave the day after tomorrow, first thing in the morning." Walker stared into Elizabeth's face, as if all had been decided.

Apparently, it had been.

"Excellent. I will work with Quill Driver and Drew to bring all the material here. Bede can then divide it between what is of interest to me and what should go with the Scribe." Papa huffed a little dominance-establishing breath.

Maybe it was better to allow him to save face now. A defeated dragon was a cranky, resentful one. Men were little different.

"Do it quickly. We do not have the luxury of time. As Walker said," Elizabeth glared at Walker from the side of her eye, "we will leave no later than the day after tomorrow, and there is a great deal to be done."

"Send someone over to Middleset House, Lizzy, to manage my packing and whatever else needs to be done, yes? And you," Papa pointed at Chisholm, "take me to Bede, so I can explain to her what needs to be done."

Elizabeth nodded to Chisholm, who led Papa from the office. "Are you comfortable with these plans, Lady Astrid?"

"Should I be?" Her entire face frowned in deep creases while her shoulders drooped. "But what choice have we when there is so much at stake?"

JUST AFTER DAWN, ALISTER Salt pulled his fine traveling coach up to the front of the Blue Order offices. "Are you sure you want to stop here?" he asked as he pulled the door open and dropped the steps.

"Yes, I am not going to slink off into the night like prey." Elizabeth tossed her head as she descended, a bulky grey bundle under her arm, and knocked on the imposing Order-blue door.

A liveried servant opened the door and gasped. "Lady Elizabeth?"

"Do not keep me waiting in the cold. Let me in." She pushed past him into the entry hall and waited for him to unlock the inner passage.

"Do you wish your presence announced? To whom?"

"No need." She strode past him. Word of her arrival would circulate soon enough.

She marched to her office and opened the door halfway. The door had so recently been installed—what a shame to hide it away.

She opened the parcel under her arm and shook out a worn grey cloth. With a flourish, she tossed it over the top of the door and smoothed it down, then closed the door firmly. The grey cloth fluttered and stilled, blanketing the door in a silent shroud that made a loud statement.

"The Dragon Sage is no longer in residence," she said to no one in particular.

In less than an hour, everyone in the office would know what had transpired, and what would happen, would happen without her. At least for now.

The same slack-jawed servant attended her exit through the front doors, closing them only when the carriage door had shut behind her.

"What did they say?" Papa asked.

"Who? What did who say?" Bede looked from Papa to her and back again.

"Nothing and no one. I spoke to no one, so whatever is said will not be said to me. I am for Pemberley."

As if on cue, Alister Salt eased the carriage toward home.

Epilogue

ALISTER SALT STOPPED THE carriage several hours out of London to change horses. Odd. They paused not at a coaching inn, but at a modest estate that Elizabeth did not recognize. A groom met them with a pair of large minor drakes. The horses remained behind with the groom while the dappled brown drakes took over, pulling the coach.

Dragons pulling a carriage? Such a thing was simply not done. Surely Alister Salt had not planned this!

No, Brutus and Walker had overseen the arrangements on their own authority. No warm-blooded officer of the Order, nay, no member of the Order could have conceived of such a thing!

All of Elizabeth's protests—and Papa's, though none of the dragons in question seemed to pay him much mind—came to naught. The drakes themselves insisted it was their privilege to serve the Dragon Sage in such a capacity and refused to allow a team of horses to take their places.

Alister Salt found it the greatest honor in the world to have dragons pulling his coach, loudly praising the team as they drove. Mortified, Papa shrank back in his seat, pulled his hat down low, and appeared to sleep.

Bede, though, chattered incessantly, remarking on the novelty of the event, and pondered the meaning of it all. Was it because of Pemberley's affinity for minor dragons that the drake team acted so? Or had the minor dragons of England found a fresh hope in Elizabeth that they had not known before, now going to extraordinary lengths to ensure her continuance in her role?

What an amazing and uncomfortable thought. One Elizabeth would have to consider further—after they completed their journey, and she could discuss the matter more freely with those who had arranged it.

While it might not be true for all drakes, these drakes, and the pairs that replaced them that evening, and the next day, had greater strength and stamina than horses, as well as the ability to see clearly in the full moon's light. They traveled through the night, making good time to Pemberley, arriving the following afternoon. Nearly as fast as a mail coach, but in much greater comfort.

Even Papa, for whom travel was a severe trial, pronounced the experience 'not too dreadful'—despite his mortification at the drakes' service. When they pulled up to Pemberley's front door, two servants arrived with a Bath chair to help him into the house.

Mrs. Sharp followed Papa out, with Little Anne sleeping on her shoulder. May, Mercy, and Truth had opted to ride outside the carriage, atop one of the trunks, additional lookouts to supplement Brutus, Axel, Kingsley, and Sergeant. Were so many guards, not to mention the dragons who drew the coach, really necessary?

All told, she did not want an answer to that question.

Drew and Chisholm half-ushered, half-pulled Bede out next. Thank heavens! Her prattle had filled the coach her every waking moment. At least her favorite topic, debating theories of translation with Papa, had kept both of them occupied and did not demand Elizabeth's participation in the discussion. And she had actually learned a great deal about the translation process, which was more interesting than she would have expected. Mrs. Sharp had actually seemed attentive, as well, almost as if she intended to incorporate some of that information into her tutelage of Little Anne and the future Baby Darcy.

Dragon's blood and bones. It was good to be home again.

She closed her eyes and sighed in the solitude. It had been less than a day and a half in the coach—half the time that would have been spent if any other coach and coachman had been employed, but still a very long time to be in less-than-ideal company. So very much company. But she was home now, and everything would be right again.

Footsteps rattled the carriage steps and the entire equipage swayed with the weight of another—person? Yes, those were warm-blood sounds. A large, familiar person dropped into the seat beside her.

"Drive on, Salt." Darcy! Oh, merciful heavens, it was him!

"Where to, Sir Fitzwilliam?"

"If your team is amenable, take the long drive around the estate."

"Very good, sir."

A warm, heavy arm slipped over her shoulder and she leaned into him, eyes still closed, savoring the scents of him: soap, shaving oil, a bit of musk. Perfect, simply perfect.

A suffocating blanket of all things burdensome and awful slipped away. She all but floated, light-headed and giddy in its absence.

"I will not ask if it was pleasant travel, for I am quite sure I know the answer." He kissed the top of her head.

"I am sorry to bring Papa and Bede."

"Walker explained it all to me. It was the right thing, given that you had no other options. We will make a way." He pulled her closer still. "Mrs. Reynolds has readied a suite of rooms near the library for him and Bede. Drew will have the option of quarters among the servants, if he would rather—"

"Oh, he would rather! He ran with the guard drakes until the final leg of today's journey."

"That is a strong statement for such a bookish dragon. I will suggest Ring personally invite him for a drink tonight."

"He will appreciate that. Will he have a seat at the table with the dragon staff as well?"

"Dale, Mrs. Reynolds' Friend, has made the arrangements and will attend to Drew's needs. Your father will have the option of having his meals brought upstairs to him so that he does not need to brave the stairs, although if you prefer—"

"I think those are ideal accommodations for him. Since Mama has been away from London, he takes all of his meals in his book room or his Order office. I have wondered if he was lonely that way, but Drew assures me he is quite content with the arrangement."

"A Bath chair and manservant have been acquired for his comfort, though I realize he may well refuse both. A team has arranged to see to Bede's needs as well, and offer supervision as necessary."

"You have thought of everything and made it all come to pass. You are truly a wonder." She cuddled into him, floating on the soothing bass of his voice.

The coach dipped slightly as it crossed a rut in the road. How strange it was to move without the sound of hooves to accompany the turn of the wheels. Dragon paws moved almost silently over the road.

"Hardly. I regret having suggested you go to London in the first place."

"I suppose one cannot be right all the time, can one?"

"One can try. I am not sorry you are home." He kissed the top of her head again.

"Dare I ask?" She opened one eye and looked up at him.

"No, nothing like that. It is simple selfishness. I missed you, and Pemberley missed you. It is not really home without you."

"Nor is London home without you. I suppose it was best that I went. I can only imagine the situation for Papa and Lady Astrid, had we not been there." She shook away the twitchy feeling in the back of her neck. "How is Pemberley? How much does she know about the situation?"

"Far more than you or I would prefer." He stretched out his legs and sighed. "She spent a significant amount of time with Cownt Matlock this summer, remember?"

"You do not mean that Matlock has brought little Pemberley into matters which are so much beyond her?"

"It is a compliment to her that Matlock would see that she is properly informed. Her rank and ours suggest she is destined for an important role in the Order. You will be very proud of her. She is working with the Viscount Andrew, Matlock's least favorite junior Keeper, and Richard's least favorite sibling." Was it possible to hear Darcy roll his eyes? "And Undersecretary Mr. St. John, in his quest to make Andrew into an acceptable Keeper and Matlock a well-run Keep."

"Did you approve that?" She pulled back and caught his gaze. "She is too young to be exposed to such a man—Andrew, I mean, not Mr. St. John, although I have no great opinion of him, either."

"My opinion was not sought." And, given his expression, he was none too happy about that, either. "But it would have matched yours, had I been asked. Oddly enough, we both would have been wrong. Pemberley has learned a great deal from trying to teach Andrew about his role as junior Keeper. Believe it or not, he seems to be responding to her far more favorably than he ever responded to Matlock."

"I notice that you did not say the viscount had learned anything, only that he responded well."

"One cannot have everything." He shrugged. "But maybe in time, Pemberley will be able to reform even him. It would certainly be for the good of everyone involved."

"At least for Matlock."

"No, my dear, far more than that. Pemberley has absolutely risen to the occasion. You will be proud of how she has matured even in the short months that you have been away."

"But it all seems too much to ask. Not just of Pemberley, but of us all. Should not Cownt Matlock, and Lord Matlock for that matter, manage these matters themselves, not sloughing off responsibility onto others? Much less a baby like Pemberley. With an attitude like that, I dread to think what they might demand of Little Anne and Bennet—"

"Bennet?" Darcy's brow drew up in a dear little wrinkle, and he cocked his head.

"Yes, Bennet. April and May have both assured me I am carrying our son." She placed Darcy's hand over her swelling belly, and Baby Darcy kicked as though he recognized his father's presence.

"A son. We are to have a son." A smile, bright as the noonday sun, blossomed across Darcy's face. "As long as you both are safe and well, I am content with whoever this baby is to be."

"You know a boy might make things complicated—he will be regarded as the heir, though Pemberley may decide—"

"That, my dearest, is a problem for another day, is it not?" Clouds parted to allow a sunbeam to peek through the sideglass. He leaned down and kissed her. Hopefully, that was the first of many to make up for lost time.

"I cannot believe I just heard you say that." She cupped his cheek with her hand.

"It surprises me, too." He laughed, and he kissed her palm. "But maybe it is not a bad thing to just enjoy these rare moments when things are not complicated."

He was right. They needed to celebrate the simple moments. For where there were dragons, complications would always abound.

OTHER BOOKS BY MARIA GRACE

World Wrights Series:
Wrighting Old Wrongs

Jane Austen's Dragons Series:
Pemberley: Mr. Darcy's Dragon
Longbourn: Dragon Entail
Netherfield: Rogue Dragon
A Proper Introduction to Dragons
The Dragons of Kellynch
Kellynch: Dragon Persuasion
Dragons Beyond the Pale
Dragon Keepers' Cotillion
The Turnspit Dragon
Dragons of Pemberley
Miss Georgiana and the Dragon
Here There Be Dragons

Secrets of the Dragon Archives

The Queen of Rosings Park Series:
Mistaking Her Character
The Trouble to Check Her
A Less Agreeable Man

Sweet Tea Stories:
A Spot of Sweet Tea: Hopes and Beginnings
Snowbound at Hartfield
A Most Affectionate Mother
Inspiration

Darcy Family Christmas Series
Darcy & Elizabeth: Christmas 1811
The Darcy's First Christmas
From Admiration to Love
Unexpected Gifts

Given Good Principles Series:
Darcy's Decision

The Future Mrs. Darcy
All the Appearance of Goodness
Twelfth Night at Longbourn

Fine Eyes and Pert Opinions
Remember the Past
The Darcy Brothers

Regency Life (Nonfiction) Series:
A Jane Austen Christmas: Regency Christmas
Traditions
Courtship and Marriage in Jane Austen's World
How Jane Austen Kept her Cool: An A to Z History of Georgian
Ice Cream

Behind the Scene Anthologies (with Austen Variations):
Pride and Prejudice: Behind the Scenes
Persuasion: Behind the Scenes
Non-fiction Anthologies
Castles, Customs, and Kings Vol. 1
Castles, Customs, and Kings Vol. 2
Putting the Science in Fiction

Available in e-book, audiobook and paperback

About the Author

Six-time BRAG Medallion Honoree, #1 Best-selling Historical Fantasy author Maria Grace has her PhD in Educational Psychology and is a 16-year veteran of the university classroom where she taught courses in human growth and development, learning, test development and counseling. None of which have anything to do with her undergraduate studies in economics/sociology/managerial studies/behavior sciences. She pretends to be a mild-mannered writer/cat-lady, but most of her vacations require helmets and waivers or historical costumes, usually not at the same time.

She writes Gaslamp fantasy, historical romance and non-fiction to help justify her research addiction.

She can be contacted at:
author.MariaGrace@gmail.com

Acknowledgments

So many people have helped me along the journey, taking this from an idea to a reality.
Thank you to my awesome beta team for cold reading and being honest. Diana, Debbie, Linda, Maureen, and Ruth
thank you so much for catching all those typos and details that I missed!
Friends of the Blue Order, your unflagging encouragement and imagination has been inspirational.
My dear friend Cathy, my biggest cheerleader, you have kept me from chickening out more than once!

Thank you!